HIS BEST FRIEND'S GIRL

CATHRYN FOX

COPYRIGHT

Discover other titles by Cathryn Fox at www.cathrynfox.com. Please sign up for Cathryn's Newsletter for freebies, ebooks, news and contests:
https://app.mailerlite.com/webforms/landing/c1f8n1
ISBN 978-1-928056-59-1
Print ISBN 978-1-928056-76-8

1

"What I wouldn't give for a piece of that."

Skylar Redmond, owner of Sky Bar in downtown Austin, glanced at Kat Stiller, who was licking her lips and looking at Skylar's best friend like he was a fresh slab of meat and she'd just come off an all-veggie diet.

"You've got a thing for Matt?" Sky asked as she refreshed Kat's strawberry daiquiri and slid it to her from the working side of the bar.

"Yeah. He's so hot." She fanned her hand in front of her pretty face, her big green eyes wide as she admired Matt from afar. "Just look at him. All that muscle, those blue eyes, the hair and those hands. God those hands... I bet he really knows how to use them to get his kink on in the bedroom." Kat sighed and spun on her padded stool to glance around the room, one filled with hot soldiers who frequented Sky Bar on a regular basis. "Too bad he's more interested in that book he's reading than he is in getting laid."

"He's studying for his MCATs," Sky explained, stealing another glace at Matt as he focused intently on the pages in front of him, oblivious to everyone and everything around him as he huddled at the far end of the bar. She looked at the jar of peanut butter beside him. Honest to God, if he didn't start eating properly he was going to get sick. He might be crazy busy seven days a week, switching careers from an army field ambulance technician to a civilian medical doctor, but no man could live off of peanuts alone. She grabbed her iPad and punched in an order that went directly to the kitchen. When Matt wasn't in class, studying, or helping with the training of service dogs, he worked at the bar with her, and every cent he made went toward saving for med school. But as his best friend since childhood, and current boss, she was not going to let him starve.

"You think that's all it is?" Kat asked, crinkling her nose.

Pool balls banged and laughter and ribbing could be heard from a half a dozen or so ex-soldiers standing around the pool table. As Sky listened to the camaraderie among friends, she grabbed a cloth and began wiping down the glassware that Dean had brought from the dish pit out back.

"What do you mean?" Sky asked. "What else would it be?"

"I mean, maybe he's not...you know...into women." She shrugged. "Not that there is anything wrong with that. But it could account for his lack of interest."

Sky nearly burst out laughing. Kat was right, there was nothing wrong with that, but she knew Matt. In their teenage years, he was one the biggest hound dogs she knew. He and their other best friend, Caleb Roth, had to fight the girls off with a stick. Those two bad boys from the wrong side of the tracks had their pick of girls. She would know, since they all hung out in Caleb's basement and she'd accidently walked in on them with their girlfriends a time or two.

"No, you're wrong. He likes his women. Believe me, back in the day he had his fair share." Then again, Sky hadn't seen him with anyone since he returned home from his tour overseas a year ago, and plenty of girls at Sky Bar had tried to get his attention. She could only chalk up his lack of enthusiasm to the important entrance exam he was studying for. Switching careers at this point was no easy task, and everyone knew the MCATs were hard to pass, even when prepared.

Kat took a sip of her drink and toyed with her straw. "Or maybe he's already into someone else."

"Yeah, probably the girl in his anatomy book," Sky said, grinning. "That's the only action he's been getting lately." She placed the polished glass on the rack and reached for another. "Besides, I thought you and Josh Mansfield had a thing."

"Yeah, Josh is great, and we've been having some fun, but...I don't know, maybe I'm looking for something more, you know?"

"More?"

She rounded her shoulder and hugged her belly. "I think my biological clock is ticking. Every time I hold Tallulah's sweet baby girl Lexi, all I can think about is having my own child."

Sky nodded as the kitchen bell sounded behind her. "I know what you mean." She grabbed Matt's sandwich from the serving shelf and slid it down the counter to him.

It hit his textbook with a thud, and his head lifted. He took note of the sandwich, then his glance went to her. He gave her a big smile and Sky just laughed, pointed at his plate and said, "Eat."

She turned back to Kat, who was studying her carefully.

"So if you know what I mean, does that mean you want to be in a serious relationship too?" Kat asked.

"Sure," she said, then closed her mouth, not wanting to admit that she was approaching thirty and the one guy she wanted she couldn't have. But she didn't want to go down that depressing road. Instead she redirected the conversation and asked, "I take it Josh isn't the settling-down kind?"

"No, but Matt sure seems like a forever kind of guy, doesn't he?"

She turned and looked at Matt as he bit into his sandwich. He followed it with a swig of soda, then licked his fingers clean—an action that seemed to have Kat squirming on her stool. Honestly, she'd never thought about Matt in that sense before. He'd just always been Matt to her. Playful, laid-back and easygoing most times, yet serious when he needed to be, like when he was studying.

"Yeah, I guess he could be a forever kind of guy," she said with a shrug.

"You guess?" Kat arched a perfectly manicured brow. "Shouldn't you know? You are best friends, aren't you?"

"Yeah, we are."

Kat gave her a once-over, a sly smirk spreading across her face. "Unless there is something more going on between you two that I don't know about. I mean, you are constantly together and he's always giving you piggyback rides." She planted her elbow on the table and opened her palm toward the ceiling. "Like I said, he's a guy who knows how to get his kink on." She went quiet, thoughtful for a moment, then wagged her index finger back and forth between Sky and Matt. "Is there something I should know? Are you two...you know...getting your kink on?"

Sky nearly laughed again. "Hardly. We're just friends. We go way back." Matt, Caleb, her—the three musketeers. "We're not getting our..." she paused and did air quotes around the words, "...kink on."

Kat wagged her eyebrows. "But you want to, right?"

"No! And for the record I'm not into kink."

"Well I am, and I want the whole package. A good, stable guy who knows how to rock my world in the bedroom."

Sky would settle for the good, stable guy. She'd never had anyone rock her world in the bedroom, and a kind, caring man was more important to her than that. "And you think Matt is that man?"

"You tell me. You're his best friend."

"To be honest, I've never thought about Matt and marriage in the same sentence before." Nor did she ever think about Matt and kink, but for some strange reason now that Kat had planted that idea in her head, she couldn't quite seem to get it out. "I guess I just never pictured him wearing a tux and standing at the altar."

Kat frowned into her drink. "That's because you didn't see him at the wedding last year."

"What happened at the wedding?" Matt was the best man at Jenny and Ving's wedding last summer, and Sky was still upset she had to miss the ceremony. She'd come down with a serious stomach flu and no way would she fly to Mississippi under those circumstances and risk giving her germs to anyone in the bridal party. Jenny had sent her a copy of the video but she'd yet to find the time to watch it.

"He looked so good. Definitely like he *belonged* at the altar. Women were throwing themselves at him, and he was always so kind, polite and gentlemanly when he declined."

As Sky eyed Kat, and took in the gloom on her face, she guessed the girl was talking from her own personal experiences with Matt. "He's different than most guys." Kat twirled her straw around her mouth and angled her head to see him. "He's not a player, at least not anymore. And he was so fiercely protective of Jenny and Ving, making sure they had everything they needed and stayed stress free during the entire time. I just bet he'd be crazy possessive of his woman too, inside the bedroom and out." She gave a wistful sigh and added, "The stories he told at the dinner party were funny yet so sweet, you know? I really think he is the whole package."

Sky couldn't help but smile, because Kat was right. Matt was funny and sweet and extremely protective of those he cared about. With no mother to raise him and an abusive father who continuously told him he'd never amount to anything, Matt was anything but a chip off the old block. In fact, he swore he'd never be anything like his old man. He'd spent many nights sleeping in Caleb's basement when his father went on a rampage. Caleb's parents might not have had much to offer, but they opened their hearts to Matt and gave him whatever they could.

"Kat?" she asked, unable to get Kat's assessment of Matt out of her head.

"Yeah."

"What makes you think Matt is into kink?"

A small, knowing smile curled up her lip. "I have a knack for these things, and believe me, he's the kind of guy who knows how to hold a girl down hard and give it to her good."

Oddly enough, a fine shiver moved through Sky, even though she wasn't into that kind of thing. In an effort to disguise her sudden interest, she pointed to the door when it opened. "Tallulah and Garrett are here."

Kat smiled and waved Tallulah over as her husband, Garrett, made his way to the pool table. Like Sky and Matt, Tallulah and Kat also went way back to childhood. Kat had only recently moved to Austin and started working at the hospital as a physical therapist so the two could be closer—and also because, according to her, the guys were way hotter in Texas.

Garrett joined his comrades as Sky went to work on making Tallulah a daiquiri. Tallulah slid onto the stool next to Kat. "What's up?" she asked. "You two looked like you were in a serious conversation."

Kat twisted on her stool and gestured with a nod toward the end of the bar. "Oh, I was just questioning Matt's sexual preferences."

"His sexual preferences?" Tallulah's dark lashes blinked

rapidly as she rolled her eyes. "Is this because he never paid you a lick of attention at the wedding last year and keeps himself holed up in that corner studying?"

"Can we not talk about Matt and licking in the same sentence?" Kat groaned. "And if you want to know the truth, then yes, it is because of that. No matter how hard I tried, I could not get that man's attention." She frowned. "I'm starting to think I'm losing it."

Sky looked at the flamboyant, gorgeous woman with the long, thick, chestnut hair that never went frizzy in Austin's humid weathers. "Losing it? Hardly. You're gorgeous, Kat. I wish I had..."

Her words fell off as the heavy oak door opened once again and Caleb Roth sauntered in. Sky's body warmed all over when he shot her a panty-dropping smile that traveled all the way to her toes, stopping in a few erogenous areas along the way. Unable to help herself, she let her gaze slide downward to take in his easy gait and the familiar way he kicked out his long legs with the same lazy ease Sky remembered from their youth. When Caleb had joined the army years ago, he left their hometown of Austin a boy, but he came back a man. A hot, sexy man who would never think of her as anything more than the pigtailed tomboy who used to climb trees with him and Matt.

"Ah, Sky..."

"What?" she asked, turning back to her friends as they both looked at her with wide-eyed curiosity. She resumed wiping down the glasses, busying her hands and pretending Caleb's mere presence hadn't thrown her off her game.

Tallulah tapped a manicured finger on the oak bar top. "Don't *what* us."

Sky reached for another glass, avoiding Tallulah's raised eyebrows. "Meaning?"

"Meaning, what the hell was that all about?" Tallulah asked.

"I'll tell you what that's all about," Kat piped in. "Sky here has the hots for Caleb."

Tallulah's brown eyes widened. "Oh my God, it's true, isn't it? When did this happen? Tell me everything."

"What's true?" Amber, Sky's head waitress and good friend, asked as she came back to the counter with her tray in hand.

Sky's mind raced as three sets of eyes stared at her. She could lie, but what was the point? They'd all see through it anyway. "Okay, fine, it's true. I have the hots for Caleb. It started when he returned home from overseas last year. There, I said it. Are you happy?"

"Like hell I'm happy," Amber said, planting one hand on her hip in usual Amber fashion. For a minute Sky thought Amber was upset because *she* wanted Caleb but then her friend's lips quirked and she pointed a finger directly at Mr. Hottie himself as he walked over to talk to Matt. "I'll be happy when you go over there and do something about it."

"No way." Sky grabbed Amber's wrist and lowered her hand as she shot Kat a glance. "You're not the one losing it, Kat. I am." She gave a disgruntled shake of her head. "Honest to God, I swear the only way I can get a guy to look at me is to tie a pork chop around my neck."

Her friends laughed and she couldn't help but laugh along with them, even though it was the sad truth. She hadn't been with a guy in ages, and if things didn't pick up soon, she was going to give up hope and start hoarding cats.

Then again, it wasn't like she'd been putting herself out there. After finishing four years of college, switching from an English degree to a business degree so she could successfully take over her father's bar when he suddenly passed away from a heart attack a few years back, all she did was work. Her mom died during childbirth and it had been just her and her father growing up. They were very close and keeping the bar a success was important to her. Not only because it was his pride and joy and he'd named it after her, but because he'd entrusted her with it. That meant everything to her. Someday down the road she could get her English degree and write the book she always wanted to, but right now she needed to put all her energy into the bar and making it a success.

Her heart ached as she thought more about her late father, who she missed dearly. He was one of a kind: smart, successful...a man who started out working in the dish pit, saving every penny he had until he could buy the bar and make it his own. He was kind, giving and cared a great deal about others, even offering his friends odd jobs when they were down on their luck. Her whole life she knew she wanted to marry a man who was as compassionate as her father.

She stole a quick glance at Caleb as he walked to the pool table and picked up a stick. She suspected he was that man. He'd come from very little and had worked hard to get where he was. Now he was an army doctor working up in the San Antonio clinic, giving back to the community and caring for the sick. He usually traveled to Austin on the weekends to hang out with her and Matt. When the weather was good and everyone could get the time off, they all often took off to his cottage at the lake.

"If you like him, then do something about it," Kat said, like it was just so simple. If only it were. "Wouldn't it be worse if you never tried?"

Sky lowered her voice, not wanting anyone to overhear them, even though no one else was sitting near them at the bar and Matt was at the other end, out of earshot. The last thing she wanted was for Matt to know how much she wanted their other best friend and make him feel like the third wheel, uncomfortable and out of place.

"He doesn't see me as anything more than a friend," Sky said. "And he never will. He still calls me Skywalker. As in Luke Skywalker. You know, like I'm one of the guys."

Tallulah leaned to her side and nudged Kat with her shoulder. "Then make him see you as a girl." She shared a smirk with Kat, like the two had a dirty little secret. "Believe me, if anyone can school you on seduction and teach you how to get a guy to notice you as something more, it's our Kat here."

Kat grinned. "You're not opposed to bending over a lot, are you?"

Sky sucked in a quick breath as her mind envisioned her doing just that. God, how naughty, wicked and...*kinky* that sounded. "You're joking, right?" Sky asked. Both girls knew her well enough to know she wasn't bold, like Kat, and had never come right out and seduced a guy before. But dammit, she was tired of going unnoticed.

"No. You have a great ass and it's time he knew it." Kat slid a napkin across the bar top. "Go over to the pool table and drop this in front of him. When you bend to pick it up, be sure to arch your back and let that little skirt you're wearing ride up." Kat winked. "Then you'll have him right where you want him. And believe me, girlfriend—" she snapped her fingers, "—he'll be hard as that stick he's holding."

Sky laughed along with her friends. While that sounded devious, and getting him hard would be nice, she truly wanted him to like her for more than her "great ass". She wanted what Kat wanted and Tallulah had—a forever kind of guy— because settling down with a family someday sounded just about right. While sex was nice, it wasn't her main priority. Finding the right man to settle down with was.

"Well, are you going to go for it?" Tallulah asked.

Sky let loose a long, slow breath and planted her hands on

the bar top. "So let me get this straight. You want me to go over to the pool table, drop this napkin, and bend over to show off my ass because you think that's what it's going to take to get Caleb to finally notice me as something more than his tomboy friend."

All three girls inched back a bit, a strange look coming over their faces. Kat and Tallulah turned their attention to their drinks and Amber scurried off to attend a table.

"What?" Sky asked, wondering if she'd said something offensive. Then again, that whole scandalous setup was *their* idea, not hers, so she had no clue as to why they were all of a sudden acting aloof.

"Thanks for the sandwich," Matt said from behind her, his mouth near her ear, his warm breath fanning over her skin.

She spun around and when she came face-to-face with her childhood best friend, she knew in an instant he'd overheard their private conversation.

With an almost tortured look on his face, Matt looked down and said, "I...ah...I think you dropped something."

She followed his gaze to the floor to find the napkin lying across her shoes like it was some clandestine clue in a secret, devious plot—which of course it was.

And now Matt knew about it!

2

Matt adjusted his backpack over his shoulder and swallowed down the lump pushing into his throat as he took note of the pink flush staining Sky's cheeks. With embarrassment written all over her face, she opened her mouth and closed it again, her expressive eyes portraying her mortification.

Coming to her rescue, he worked to keep things light and hurried out with, "Caleb wants to hit up a movie so I'm going to take off for a bit."

"You finished studying?" she said breezily, but he could tell she was struggling to follow his lead and keep the conversation casual.

"For now. Doctor's orders." He gestured toward Caleb as he put his cue stick away and started toward them. "But I'll be back before closing to help you lock up."

In a swift move she kicked the napkin away, like she was trying to dispose of evidence. Her friends kept one eye on their drinks and the other on them as they pretended not to eavesdrop.

"You don't have to do that." Sky smoothed her hand

through her shoulder length blonde hair. She pushed the strands off her face, only for them to recoil back in place when she let them go. With obstinate resolve written all over her, she jutted her chin out. "I'm quite capable of locking up myself."

"Yeah, yeah, I know," he said. He also knew *independent* was her middle name—so was *stubborn*. She'd been that way her whole life. Little tomboy Sky might have been a tough kid growing up—compliments of having no mother, something they both shared—but she was also kind, and the only girl in the neighborhood he and Caleb allowed into the half-assed tree house they'd built in Caleb's yard. Regardless, tenacious or not, there had been a rash of break-ins around the neighborhood lately, and the bar wasn't in the best part of town, which meant he didn't want her walking to their apartment building alone, no matter how capable she was. Plus, that asshole Simon Harris was here drinking with his construction crew tonight, and he didn't trust the guy or like the way he looked at Sky. "But I have to check on Gran's house anyway." He liked to do a perimeter check every night and make sure she'd set the security alarm before going to sleep. "And it's on the way to our place." Well, technically it wasn't their place. They lived in the same apartment complex, not the same apartment.

As she stood there staring up at him like she was waiting for him to say more, the full impact of her admission suddenly hit like a sucker punch. Christ, how could he possibly be expected to keep the conversation going—not to mention his shit together—after hearing what she planned to do to with that damn napkin. With Caleb. But now that she'd said it, put her feelings for their other best friend right out there in the open, there was one thing he did know. He could no longer ignore it.

No, he could no longer overlook the way she acted when

Caleb was around. The way she all of a sudden started staring at him differently and touching him more frequently, letting her fingers linger on his arm, his leg, his face more than she used to.

Fuck.

Sky knew he'd overheard them, which meant they'd have to eventually talk about it. Hell, they talked about everything else under the sun, everything except how she really felt about their best friend. But he didn't need to hear her voice the word to know what was going on with her, or how perfect his two best childhood friends would be together.

Caleb was a good guy and had a lot to offer, and, honestly, he wanted only what was best for Sky. That's all he'd ever wanted. Even though he'd been in love with her since the first time she skinned her knee on the playground, then threw a little dirt on it instead of crying, he understood he, Matt James—a guy who barely finished high school and took a front-line, expendable position in the army—was not the guy for her. No, she deserved someone better. Someone like Caleb.

What the hell did he have to offer a girl like her, anyway? Not a goddamn thing. At least not until he completed his medical degree, and he wasn't even sure he could pass the entrance test. He scoffed. Maybe on some deeper level he'd changed paths because he figured if he ever amounted to more he might actually be worthy of her. But none of that mattered now, because her feelings for Caleb were clear and he wouldn't do a damn thing to stand in their way.

"Matt…" she began, then stopped talking when Caleb leaned over the counter and tugged her hair.

"Hey, Skywalker," he said, a warm, familiar lilt to his voice as he called her by her childhood nickname.

"Caleb," she responded as he flashed a charming smile her way. Matt shook his head. He loved Caleb like a brother, would take a bullet for him, but damned if the man couldn't charm the bite off a snake.

Sky turned from Caleb to Matt, her eyes pleading. His heart hitched. Jesus, she was so perfect, and so beautiful. She had an innocent sensuality about her that she had no idea she possessed. But she was soon going to be his best friend's girl, he quickly reminded himself. So it was hands off from here on out.

"Matt," she murmured in a breathless whisper.

Wanting her to know her secret was safe with him, Matt put his mouth near her ear and whispered, "We'll talk later." Unable to help himself, he breathed in her sweet smell, and when her hair brushed over his face, he stifled a groan. His mind instantly envisioned her splayed out on his bed, pinned beneath his body, screaming out *his* name as he pounded into her with long, hard strokes that would make her forget her own. He coughed to hide the things he was feeling, then straightened to look at Caleb. "Ready?" he asked.

"Wait, aren't you coming?" Caleb asked Sky.

"No, I can't."

Matt frowned. He really wished she'd kick back and find time for herself more often, but she'd given her assistant manager the night off, which meant the responsibility of locking up rested with her.

"Why not?" Caleb asked.

Sky waved her hand around the bar. "I have to work."

Caleb fished his keys from his pocket. "Aw, come on. You know what they say about all work and no play."

"That's right," Matt said.

She punched Matt in the arm. "You're one to talk."

Slipping into play mode, Matt grabbed her arms and pinned them behind her back. "Are you saying I'm dull?"

She wiggled and her body pressed against his. Their groins collided and when his cock thickened he realized what he was doing. It was time to stop playing with Sky...time to stop touching her and thinking about her as anything other than a friend.

Caleb twirled his key chain around his finger. "At least tell me you're free next weekend." Next weekend Caleb would be leaving his twenties behind. Two weeks after that, Matt would be saying farewell to his.

Matt let her hands go and stepped back, working to get his shit together when she grinned at Caleb, a gleam in her eyes. "I wouldn't miss your thirtieth birthday for the world, Caleb."

Caleb eyed her. "Ah, should I be scared? You look like you have something on your mind."

"I just thought a little payback was in order."

"Payback?" Caleb's curious glance went from Sky, to Matt back to Sky again. "What the hell you talking about?"

"You don't remember putting me over your knee and spanking me twenty-nine times on my birthday last year?"

Caleb's grin returned. "Ah, I think you had one too many celebratory drinks, Skywalker. It was Matt who held you down and spanked you, not me."

"Oh," she said, her eyes going wide as she looked at Matt. When their gazes met and locked, something strange moved over her face, something he couldn't quite identify, and that was saying a lot, considering she was such an easy read to him.

"And just for the record—" Caleb pointed a finger at Matt, "—he was also the one who put the icing on your nose, not me. So don't get any ideas."

Matt shrugged and walked around the bar. "Gran's old tradition."

Kat cleared her throat and when all eyes turned to her, Kat zeroed in on Sky. Her lips curled up at the corners, like she and Sky knew a secret. "Spankings and icing." She took a long pull from her straw, then said, "Imagine that." She turned to Tallulah. "Can't wait for my birthday."

Caleb turned his attention to the two women grinning at each other. "You two are coming, right?"

"I'll be there," Kat said.

Tallulah nodded. "Babysitter is already booked."

Matt checked his watch and started toward the door. "Come on, movie is starting soon."

"Okay, see you later, Skywalker," Caleb said, turning to follow Matt outdoors.

Matt looked at his friend, his comrade, his brother in crime, and couldn't help but want to know how he felt about Sky. He couldn't come right out and ask because he didn't want to betray her trust. He'd promised her that her secret was safe with him, and he'd never, ever go back on a promise. Still a little subtle investigation couldn't hurt, right?

A car door slammed and sexy Daisy, who hung out at the bar, hiked her purse over her shoulder and started toward them. Dressed in her usual frayed short shorts and cowgirl boots that climbed up her long legs, she cut through the parking lot.

Caleb made a noise. "I wouldn't mind unwrapping that sweet thing for my thirtieth."

"Hi, boys," Daisy said, doing a sexy little finger wave as she sauntered by, giving an extra shake to her hips when she saw the way Caleb was looking at her.

Matt jumped into the passenger seat of Caleb's SUV and tossed his backpack onto the seat beside him. He looked through the passenger side window and watched Daisy until she disappeared inside the bar. "Yeah, she's hot. But you're getting old, man." He put his hand on Caleb's head and gave a little shove. "Time to start thinking with your head, and as sweet as Daisy is, she's not the marrying type."

"What the hell?" Caleb shot him a quick glance then

turned the engine over in his vehicle. "Marrying type? Christ, Matt, you need to stop hanging around Gran so much. You sound like a seventy-year-old woman. And besides, I'm only turning thirty. That doesn't mean life stops and I have to get hitched. And you know we're the same age. You're only two weeks behind."

Caleb pulled out into traffic and drove toward the theater. "So do you ever think about finding the right girl and settling down?" Matt asked.

"You're channeling Gran again." Caleb laughed and eyed him. "What's gotten into you, anyway?" Caleb reached across the cab to touch Matt's forehead. "You getting your period?"

"Fuck off," Matt said, pushing his hand away. Okay, maybe he needed to cool it on all the "girl" talk before Caleb demanded he turn in his man card. "I think I've just had my head in a book too long."

"I think you need to get laid, pal."

"Maybe you're right." As they parked and bought their tickets to the movie, Matt gave more consideration to the long dry spell he was in. The truth was, it was hard to climb between the sheets and have casual sex when all he could think about was Sky. She'd given him a job when he returned home from overseas last year, and being around her every day was really playing havoc with his head—both of them. But fuck, now that he knew the truth, he needed to move on and forget about her. Maybe after the flick he'd go find Daisy. She'd come on to him a time or two before and he'd politely declined, but maybe next time he wouldn't say no. Yeah, maybe next time he'd take her home and show her that he was anything but a gentleman behind closed doors.

With his thoughts too preoccupied with other things, Matt could barely concentrate on the movie, but forced a laugh during the appropriate times, otherwise Caleb would pick up on his unease and grill the shit out of him.

When the lights came on, Caleb stretched and looked at his watch.

"You crashing at my place?" Matt asked, climbing to his feet.

"Nah, I think I'll head back to San Antonio tonight."

"Yeah?" They followed the crowd out the doors and the warm night air fell over them as they walked back to the SUV. "I thought you didn't work tomorrow."

Caleb grinned. "I don't. But there is a cute new nurse in the clinic. She messaged me earlier and mentioned something about an anatomy lesson." He laughed. "You know me, I like to help out where I can."

Matt laughed along with his friend, even though he was cringing inside. He hopped into the truck and rested his hand on his backpack.

"You want me to drop you off at Gran's?" Caleb asked, pulling in to traffic.

"No, Sky Bar."

He glanced at the dashboard clock as he drove the short distance to the bar. "Isn't it closed?"

"I told Sky I'd help her lock up." Matt stared straight ahead but could feel Caleb's eyes on him. They turned down the street and he could see Sky Bar in the distance. "What?" Matt finally asked.

"I don't know. What's going on with you? You seem fucked up about something. You want to talk about it?"

"Now who's got their period?" Matt said. He pointed to the bar's back parking lot. "Pull in there." When the truck stopped, Matt opened his door, and before Caleb could continue with his interrogation and possibly squeeze the truth from him, he said, "I'll catch up with you next weekend at the cottage."

"You taking your bike down, or are you catching a ride with Sky?"

He opened his mouth to tell him he'd ride to the cottage with Sky, but then quickly changed his mind. The less time he spent in enclosed spaces with her the better, and he always enjoyed the long ride on his motorcycle.

"I'll take the bike."

"I don't work Friday so why don't we head down early?" Caleb asked.

"Okay, see you then."

"Tell Sky if she wants to come with me in the truck to save gas, there's plenty of room."

"Will do."

Matt closed the door, adjusted his backpack over his shoulder, and looked around the empty parking lot as he made his way to the back door. He fished his key from his pocket and let himself in. Music from Sky's father's prized jukebox reached his ears as he entered. The tunes drowned out his footsteps as he pushed the chairs into the tables and made his way down the long hall to her office.

When he spotted her, tapping away on her computer, a faraway look on her face, his throat tightened. He could only guess she was dabbling with one of her stories. Sky longed to be a writer, but had put that dream on hold to run her father's business. Matt just wished she'd sell half of the business to her assistant manager, Marco, like Marco had been asking her to do for years. At least that would cut back on the hours she had to spend here, freeing her up to fulfill her dreams and take some of the burden off her shoulders.

She never talked about her writing anymore, but Matt knew the dream still lived within her. As he watched, he wondered if she was visualizing Caleb as her hero. Caleb, who was currently off playing doctor with some nurse while Sky sat here trying to figure out a way to get his attention. Not that Matt could blame Caleb for doing what came natural to any hot-blooded male. Caleb was single, had no one to answer to and had no idea how Sky felt about him. It sure as hell wasn't Matt's place to tell him.

She blinked thick lashes over tired brown eyes, and her hair fell forward, wild and untamed. His fingers itched to grab a fistful and tug as he planted his mouth on hers. What he'd do to give her a hot, hard kiss that told her in no uncertain terms to forget about Caleb and start noticing him. But he wouldn't do that, because he had nothing to offer but a good time between the sheets.

Exhaling slowly to pull himself together, he dug his phone from his pocket. Not wanting to startle her, he swiped the screen and sent her a message.

"I'm here."

Her phone pinged and vibrated on the desk. She picked it up, ran her fingers over the screen and texted back. "I'm in the office."

"I know."

Her head inched up and when her eyes met his, a huge smile split her lips. "Hey, you. How was the movie?" She looked past his shoulders like she was searching for Caleb and he tried not to show a reaction.

"Good," he said. "You all set?"

She closed her laptop. "Yeah."

Matt gestured with a nod to her computer as she packed it away in her case. "What were you doing?"

"Just paying bills."

Matt nodded but didn't push the matter as she stacked paper on her desk and started to clean up. From the wistful look on her face, he guessed she wasn't paying bills at all, and the girl couldn't tell a fib if her damn life depended on it. He grinned, thinking back to their teen years when they all drank too much and crashed in Caleb's basement. She'd been so sick that night. He and Caleb had spent the better part of the night taking turns holding her hair as she hovered over the toilet. She'd told her father she stayed at some girlfriend's house and was too sick to call because she had the flu. He saw right through that lie, and accused her of being out with a boy. But she hadn't been out with just one boy. She'd been out with two. Her father wasn't half as angry when he found out Sky had been with him and Caleb. He shook his head as he thought about that. He and Caleb had a reputation a mile long. Why her father had ever trusted her with the likes of them, he'd never know.

Matt played with his key inside his pocket and leaned against the doorjamb as he waited. Sky grabbed her purse from the drawer and met up with him. Everything in the way she moved was so sexy, so sensuous, he had no idea how Caleb couldn't see that she was all grown up.

An easy silence fell over them as they stepped outside and Matt wondered if she was going to bring up what he'd overheard. He locked up and they walked toward Gran's house. Gran was his mom's mother. He lost his mom to cancer when he was just a toddler, so he didn't know Gran very well growing up, and had been working hard to make up time ever since. She'd moved here to take over his father's house a few years back when his dad had died. Matt didn't want anything to do with the house. It held nothing but bad memories and he preferred to live in his little one-bedroom apartment across the hall from Sky. It wasn't much of an apartment, but it was a place to lay his head nonetheless.

"How's Gran?" Sky asked and Matt knew she was hedging.

Matt kicked a rock and slowed his pace so she could keep up. "Good. She'd probably like to see you soon. It's been a while."

"I know. I've just been so busy at work." Silence, and then, "Matt?"

"Hmmm."

"About what you overheard," Sky began, crinkling her nose as she lifted her chin to meet his eyes.

"Yeah. I thought you might want to talk about it."

"I didn't mean for you to hear any of it."

They moved down the sidewalk and a car sped by, the passengers in the backseat hollering out to Sky. This, of course, was why he liked to walk her home. Sure, they didn't live far and she could take care of herself, but there were assholes everywhere and he'd been protecting her from them for as long as he could remember.

"I know," he said, wishing he hadn't heard it too. But he had and now he couldn't ignore it.

She tucked her hair behind her ears. "I...just..."

"So you like Caleb," he stated and rolled his shoulder casually, like there wasn't a shit storm going on inside him. "It's no big deal."

"Really?" she asked, her eyes wide. "It doesn't make you uncomfortable?"

"Why would it? Caleb's a great guy, and I think you two would be great together."

"You do?"

"Sure."

She toyed with the zipper on her purse. "Are you serious, Matt?"

"Yeah, I'm serious. You should go for it."

She looked at the ground as they walked, going quiet for a moment. "He still thinks I'm one of the guys."

"Which was why you were going to try that whole napkin thing?"

She cringed and cupped her cheeks. "Oh God, that is so embarrassing. I wasn't really going to do it, you know."

"No."

"I don't think so. Then again, maybe I was. I don't know. I'm...I'm just...not really all that noticeable."

Matt stopped and turned to her, the streetlamp overhead spilling over them. When she blinked up at him with those big brown eyes, he gripped her shoulders. How could she not see how beautiful and special she really was? "Look, Sky. You don't need tricks. You're beautiful, smart and independent. A guy would be crazy not to see that."

"Oh." She stared at him for a long moment, her eyes moving over his face like she could see right through him. He let go of her shoulders and stepped back, putting a measure of distance between them.

"Caleb's birthday is this weekend," he said quickly to distract her. "We're all heading to the cottage so maybe it's a good time to show him that you're all grown up and get him to see you as the beautiful woman you are."

What the fuck am I doing?

Her gaze fell to his chest and she looked like she was a million miles away. Then she blinked and looked back up at him. "So you really think I should go for it? You really think we'd be good together?"

"Yeah. I do," he said and started walking again. Only his footsteps echoed in the quiet night, and he could feel her gaze drilling into his back as she stood still behind him. "Coming?" he finally asked.

"You're the best friend any girl could ever have, Matt."

Before he realized what was happening, Sky jumped on his back for a piggyback ride. Her legs wrapped around his waist and as he grabbed her thighs to hoist her up, he knew he'd rather be tortured for hours by the enemy than think about her in bed with his best friend.

3

There was nothing Sky could do to fight down the jittery feeling mushrooming inside her stomach as she negotiated her car along the winding road leading to Caleb's cottage. She chose not to catch a lift with Caleb, instead deciding to drive herself, as well as Kat and Tallulah. Tallulah's husband, Garrett, would be joining them all later. A decorated ex-soldier turned cop, he now worked the beat in downtown Austin and didn't get off until after dinner. She looked at Tallulah sitting beside her, and then at Kat in the backseat. Sky didn't get out from behind the counter at the bar too often and was glad for this quiet time with the girls—before she seduced Caleb and changed the way he looked at her. She swallowed. Hard.

"Come on, Sky, everything will be fine," Tallulah said, clearly picking up on her nervousness. She clapped her hands together. "I think you and Caleb will be so good together."

Sky drove down the long road to the cottage, waving to the people jogging along the gravel road as they ran past. "We've been friends a long time. I don't want to do anything to ruin that."

"I know." Tallulah reached over and squeezed her hand. "But you won't. I'm sure of it. And like Kat said, wouldn't it be worse if you never tried?"

From the backseat Kat said, "If you do nothing at all, then you'll never know and could spend the rest of your life regretting it."

Sky turned the wheel, taking the gravel road that led to the left. "True."

"And you do owe him thirty spankings right? Talk about the perfect opening for a seduction," Kat added.

That was more along the lines of Kat's seduction. Sky's involved slipping into his bedroom in her negligee, not spankings—at least she didn't think so. She bit her bottom lip, hardly able to believe the directions of her thoughts. Up until now her sex life had been pretty vanilla, and she was happy with that. Caleb didn't strike her as the kinky kind anyway, which was just fine by her. She simply wanted a good guy and wasn't looking for anything out of the ordinary between the sheets. Nope. Stable and kind trumped a guy who would hold his girl down hard and give it to her good. *Oh my*. All Kat's talk of kink had to be getting to her.

Sky jacked the air conditioning and caught Kat's mischievous glance in the rearview mirror. "What about you, Kat?" Sky asked. "Are you going to try to get Matt to notice you?"

Kat grabbed a handful of hair, tied it up into a ponytail and gestured toward the birthday cake on the seat beside her. "As delicious as Matt and icing in the same room sounds, no. I've given up on him. This weekend is all about soaking up the rays and relaxing."

Tallulah smirked. "Yeah, and that's only because she has a hot new patient at the hospital who is in for a little physical therapy."

"Oh, and who might that be?" Sky asked. "Anyone I know?"

"If you know Thor, then yes."

"Thor?" Sky said, laughing.

"Theodore Grant. He's a friend of Garrett's. Injured in the line of duty and recently discharged," Tallulah explained.

"Thor, for short," Kat said. "At least that's what I call him, and for the record there is nothing short about him."

Sky caught Kat's glance in the mirror again. "So he's a forever kind of guy?"

Kat gave a sly smirk. "Yeah, he sure seems like he could go on forever and ever."

Everyone laughed, but Sky's smile quickly dissolved when she reached the end of the road and pulled in behind Caleb's truck. She caught sight of Matt's motorcycle parked near the shed.

"Looks like everyone is here."

She glanced around and spotted Luke and Emery kissing down by the wharf, and was happy that Luke had finally knocked the chip off his shoulder and went for what he wanted. Thinking about that had her thoughts going to Caleb and how she was about to step out of her comfort zone and go for what she wanted too. With any luck she'd also have a happy ending, because the alternative, which could very well mean putting a crimp into their friendship, was something she couldn't allow to happen.

"Show time," Kat said, and reached for her door handle. "You brought that napkin, right?"

Sky laughed. "No, I didn't."

"The napkin is a guaranteed win, Sky."

"Well I didn't bring it, so I guess I'll just have to improvise," she said, thinking about the sexy underwear she'd recently purchased.

Kat tapped the back of Sky's seat. "You know, there is one other way to get him to notice you."

"Oh?" Sky said.

"Yeah, every guy wants what other guys have," Kat said.

"Meaning?"

"Meaning, if he starts seeing another guy notice you then he'll notice you too."

"Since there are *no* other guys that notice me, that plan is out. Besides, Matt said I didn't need to use any tricks." Both Tallulah and Kat stopped cold and stared at her.

"What?" they said in unison.

"What?" Sky responded, her glance bobbing back and forth between her two friends.

"What exactly did Matt say?" Kat asked, her perceptive green eyes narrowing in on Sky's.

Feeling a little uncomfortable under her friend's scrutiny, Sky shifted in her seat. "Nothing, really. I mean we talked about what he overheard and he told me I didn't need any tricks to get a guy's attention. That any guy would be lucky to have me."

Kat let loose a long, slow whistle and gave a shake of her head like she'd just had some major epiphany. "Oh, shit. Now it all makes sense."

Sky turned in her seat and rested her hand on the passenger headrest as both Tallulah and Kat stared at her. "What are you talking about?" Sky asked, not really sure if she wanted to hear it.

"Matt. He likes you," Kat blurted out.

Sky shook her head hard at the outrageousness of that statement. "No, he doesn't," she said quickly. They were close, yes. But never once had he shown any interest in her outside of their friendship. "He was the one who encouraged me to go for it with Caleb. He told me he thought we were perfect for each other. If he liked me he wouldn't do that, right?"

"I guess you're right," Tallulah said, nodding her head in agreement.

Kat gave them both a dubious look and did some weird head-bobbing thing. "Whatever you say," she said. With cake in hand, she climbed from the car.

Sky slid from her seat and met the girls at the trunk. She popped it and they all grabbed their gear. She hiked her bag over her shoulder just as Matt came around the corner, wearing his backpack. As she looked at him, she took in the dark smudges under his eyes. He might looked relaxed in his swim trunks and T-shirt but she knew him well enough to know he was studying too much and wasn't getting enough sleep. He had never been a great student and she knew how worried he was, but this weekend he needed a break and she was damn well going to see to it that he got the rest he needed.

"Need any help?" he asked, and before Sky could answer, he grabbed her duffle bag and shouldered it.

Sky closed the trunk, and Tallulah and Kat rushed off to take their luggage inside. Matt gave her a little nudge with his shoulder to set her into motion. She followed along beside him, lost in her thoughts, her conversation with Kat still lingering in her brain.

"Hey, you okay?" Matt asked.

"Fine, why?"

"You seem a little distracted."

Gravel crunched beneath her feet as she walked and the fragrant scent from the trees and foliage fell over her as they approached the cottage's front door. She breathed in the smells of nature in an effort to relax herself, then exhaled slowly.

"Matt..." she began, thinking Kat couldn't be right. Was it possible that Matt liked her?

"Yeah?"

"You don't..." She let her words fall off and gave herself a quick lecture. Of course he didn't like her, and coming right out and asking him was only going to make things awkward between them. Refusing to let Kat's ridiculous epiphany mess with her head, she asked, "How's the studying going?"

"It's going."

She touched his arm, and he flinched like he'd been physically struck. "Whoa," she said, taken aback. "Everything okay?"

"Yeah, sorry. Just got a little too much sun today." She looked at his arm, and wondered why he was lying. "And I think I'm a little tense, worried about taking the MCATs."

"I know you are, but I think you need a break. All work and no play makes Matt a tense boy. How about this, you take some time off this weekend and when we get back to the city, I'll help you study. I told you I didn't mind."

His features softened as his gaze moved over her face. "Okay, and I really should close the books. I mean it *is* Caleb's birthday." The second Caleb's name left his mouth they both went quiet for a moment. Matt glanced over her shoulder, like he was looking for Caleb, and raked his fingers through his hair. "So why don't we go grab a beer and see what everyone is up to?"

A strange, uneasy feeling moved through her as he began to walk away from her. "Matt, wait…" He turned back to her and her stomach clenched. He was her best friend, and she needed to know he was okay with her going after Caleb. She'd never want to do anything to ruin their friendship. She'd be completely lost without him in her life. She stepped up to him. "Are you sure you're okay with—"

He cupped her face. "Sky. You two are perfect for each other. I told you that already. Caleb just doesn't know it yet." He touched his head. "Sometimes he can be pretty thick." They both shared a laugh, the tension between them easing. "You and me, we're good."

"You sure?"

"Positive. Now come on. I really need that beer."

They reached the front door and Kat and Tallulah were already in their swimsuits and headed for the water. She followed Matt inside, and he dropped their bags on the kitchen floor. He went to the fridge to grab them each a beer and Sky took that moment to wipe her suddenly damp hands on her shorts. God, she could hardly believe she was going to seduce Caleb, right here in his cottage. She looked past the kitchen counter at the sofa facing the huge widow overlooking the lake. When she spotted Caleb on his boat with fellow comrade Jack Barnes, kicking back and drinking a beer, a streak of nervousness raced through her.

Matt came up behind her, and when she caught his familiar scent of sandalwood, soap and something uniquely Matt, she was about to turn, but ended up shrieking and running from him when he lifted the back of her T-shirt and pressed the cold bottle to her skin.

She should have expected it, of course. Ever since they were kids, Matt was always carrying on with her like that, and she knew better than to turn her back on him.

"That's freezing," she cried out, spinning to face him when she was a safe distance away, happy that the tension between them was gone and he was back in play mode.

His gaze dropped from her face and traveled downward. For a minute she thought he was checking out the sliver of skin between her shorts and tank top, but then his eyes went back to hers. "You look...hot."

She caught the strange expression that came over his face before he twisted the cap off and held the bottle of beer out to her. He cleared his throat and ran a hand through his hair, messing it in that way that made him look so boyish and adorable. "I mean, you looked like you were hot. Here. Drink."

She pointed to the end table. "Put it there."

He grinned and rooted his feet. "Nope. You have to come and get it."

"You two at it again?" Jack Barnes asked as he came sauntering in through the door behind her.

"At what?" Sky said, turning to face him.

Jack rolled his eyes and grabbed a beer from the fridge. "Get a room already."

Matt turned on him and gave a razor-sharp look that would kill anything in its path. "Jack," he said through clenched teeth.

"Whoa." Jack held his hands up and backed out. "Sorry. Just kidding."

The second Jack left, Matt said, "Where are you sleeping?"

"Kat and I are going to share. We talked about it on the way here." She pointed to one of two bedrooms on the main level. One was Caleb's, and the other a spare. Up above there was a loft, but it looked like Luke and Emery had already claimed that. "Tallulah said she and Garrett are taking the boat house."

He grabbed her bag, walked to the bedroom, and tossed in onto the big bed, beside Kat's small suitcase.

"Where are you sleeping?" she asked, hoping to sound casual. Matt often crashed with Caleb in his king-sized bed, but tonight if he did that, it would certainly put a kink into her plans. *Kink?* Okay, maybe she meant *throw a monkey wrench* into her plans, because she didn't mean kink as in kinky. Jesus, why the hell was that stupid word stuck her brain?

When their eyes met, his darkened, a good sign that he knew what she was getting at. "I'm going to crash on the boat," he said, then took a long pull from his beer.

Shrieks could be heard from the lake and she turned toward the window in time to see Luke toss Emery off the dock into the water. "I think I'll get changed and go for a dip."

"Yeah, me too," Matt said. He gripped his shirt and her gaze went to his big hands as he peeled it from his shoulders, hands that had held her down and spanked her. Could Kat have been right? Could Matt be into kink? Not that she should be thinking about that. What he did behind closed doors was his business and she was here to seduce Caleb —not Matt.

———

Matt stretched out beside Caleb by the fire, watching the flames as they licked the star-studded night sky. He twirled his beer bottle in his hands and drew in a calming breath. He'd been antsy all day and after a barbecue dinner of hamburgers and hot dogs he thought about taking off and heading back to his apartment. But if he disappeared, then Sky would know something was up. What they had between them was good and he didn't want to risk losing her as a friend by letting his jealousy show. Besides, deep in his heart he knew Caleb was the right man for her.

Six of the chairs around him sat empty. Everyone had already gone to claim their room, leaving him on the boat and Jack on the sofa. Now it was just the three musketeers sitting around the fire pit. He turned to see his best friend suck back another beer. Caleb usually didn't drink much, but it was his birthday and tonight he was kicking back. Only problem was if he didn't slow down, he was going to pass out, then Sky's plan—whatever it might be—would fail, and fail hard.

He took a moment to consider that, then reached into the cooler. He drove his hand through the melting ice and produced another brew. "Here have another," he said, shoving it at Caleb.

Shit.

Just as Caleb reached for it, his conscience got the better of him and he pushed the bottle back into the cooler. He might be a lot of things, but he wasn't a total asshole.

"Actually, let's go for a swim," he said to Caleb. A good douse of cold water might help sober him up a bit.

"Nah, I'm just going to crash." Caleb set his empty bottle down and stood on wobbly legs. He took a step toward the house and damn near did a face plant. "Jesus," he said then laughed as he gripped the back of his chair for balance.

Sky stood, stretched and yawned. "I think I'll call it a night too."

Matt clenched down on his teeth hard enough to break bone and didn't meet her eyes when he said, "Yeah, same."

"Come here, Skywalker," Caleb said, and when she walked over to him, he threw his arm around her shoulder. "I'm so glad you came tonight." He put her in a headlock and ran his knuckles over her head. "I don't see enough of you anymore."

Sky punched him in the side and he let loose a loud oomph. The two laughed, then Sky slipped her arm around his waist, and Matt's gut churned as he watched them walk toward the cottage. Fuck. He grabbed the water bucket, filled it with the nearby hose, and tossed it onto the flames. Smoke billowed upward and filled the sky, but there was nothing he could do to extinguish the angry fire burning in his gut. Once the two disappeared inside, he made his way toward the boat. He could try to sleep but he knew he'd only lie there and think about what was going on inside—in Caleb's bed.

4

Sky tightened her grip on Caleb's waist as he wobbled on unsteady legs. Her stomach knotted with worry. Maybe tonight wasn't such a great night to seduce him. He'd had a lot to drink and didn't seem all that coherent. But she'd spent the better part of the week preparing for this and if she didn't do it right now, she might not ever find the courage again.

"Night, Skywalker," Caleb said when they stepped inside the quiet, dimly lit cottage. With his arm around her shoulders he pulled her closer and kissed the top of her head. He sputtered as he got a mouth full of her curls and inched back. "Catch you in the morning."

"Night," she said, removing her arm from his waist.

Caleb stepped away and gripped the wall, feeling his way along it until he reached the bathroom. He disappeared inside, and a moment later the sound of water running reached her ears. Nervous excitement nipped at her as she tiptoed to the room she was sharing with Kat. She moved quietly, stealthily, taking care not to wake Jack, who was asleep on the sofa. Although from his snoring sounds he seemed to be in a pretty deep slumber. Good. The last thing she wanted was for him to wake up and catch her sneaking in to Caleb's room in her skimpy underthings. She wasn't into exhibitionism. Kink however... Wait! What? Damn you, Kat.

The knob felt warm to her touch as she gripped it and slowly turned it. The hinges creaked and she sucked in a breath and held it. Kat was asleep inside, and she didn't want to wake her either. The moon shining in through the cracks in the curtain gave her sufficient light to root around in her bag. When her fingers connected with the lacy bra and panties she'd purchased for this seduction, she pulled them out and laid them on the bedspread.

Quiet as a church mouse, she peeled her clothes from her body, shoved them into her bag and slipped into the barely there panties, and demi bra that gave her the perfect amount of cleavage. She pressed her ear to the door and listened for movement in the cottage. A toilet flushed and a few minutes later Caleb's heavy footsteps echoed in the open cabin as he exited the bathroom and made his way to his bed.

Sky pressed her back to the door, took a fueling breath of courage and let it out slowly. There was no mirror to give herself a once-over in, so she smoothed her hand through her hair and adjusted the straps on her bra. A bout of nervousness started to get the best of her. Maybe this was a really, really bad idea. Maybe she should have gone with the napkin trick.

Her heart raced faster as she forced herself to move. She pushed off the door and slipped from the room. A rustling sound in the loft overhead had her stilling. She listened and when the noise settled down, she made her way to Caleb's closed door. She wrapped her hand around the knob and gathered her bravado.

Here goes nothing. Or...rather...everything.

———

Matt walked along the dock and ran his fingers along the metal rail on the boat as it bobbed in the light waves and brushed up against the wharf. Staring into the night, and trying to keep his mind off of what was taking place inside the cottage, he looked across the water at the chalets dotting the lake. He pulled off his shirt and, hoping a swim would exhaust him so he would fall into a deep sleep, he dove in.

Coldness enveloped him, temporarily tamping down the flames licking through his veins. He stayed under for as long as he could and surfaced a good distance from the dock. He swam long and hard, until his muscles ached and fatigue pulled at him. The lights in the cottage were out, and the area was drenched in darkness by the time he made his way back. Pushing himself from the water, he grabbed the ladder and climbed back onto the dock.

He reached for his shirt, but a sniffling sound behind him caught his attention. Turning, he found Sky sitting on the dock, her legs dangling over the side.

"Sky, Jesus, what is it?" he asked, crouching down beside her. She turned to him and his heart pinched when he saw the turmoil on her face. "Are you okay?"

She plucked at the hem of her long sweater and leaned forward, her hair falling into her face and masking her emotions. "Yes...no. I don't know."

Heart racing, Matt pushed her hair from her face and ran his thumb over her cheek. A burst of tenderness stole over him. "Hey, what is it?"

"I feel so stupid. I can't believe it." She looked skyward and shook her head. "God, how could I have been so stupid to think it would have worked."

Understanding hit. Sky was here sitting on this dock with him instead of rolling around between the sheets with Caleb. He didn't know whether to laugh or cry.

He dropped down beside her, their legs touching as he

shifted closer. He leaned into her and nudged her with his shoulder. "You want to talk about it?

"No...I don't know."

"Why don't you tell me what happened?"

"Nothing happened."

Thank fuck.

"Something must have happened." As his gaze moved over her face, he worked to dispel the image of her dressed in next to nothing and bending over to seduce Caleb. "Otherwise you wouldn't be sitting here upset." She stayed quiet. Too quiet. "Come on. Talking about it will make you feel better," he said, even though he seriously didn't want to hear the details. But she was his friend, and she obviously needed him right now. Which meant he'd have to bury his feelings so he could be there for her.

She sniffed and covered her face with her hands. "I can't. It's too embarrassing."

He reached for one hand and pitched his voice low as he pulled it from her face. "Hey, it's me, Sky."

She looked at him, and a small smile tugged at the corners of her mouth. He bent his head and his wet hair fell forward. Like she'd done on many occasions, she reached out and smoothed it back. The feel of her soft fingers rekindled that fire inside him and his cock reacted. He put his arm over his erection, not wanting her to know what her closeness was doing to him.

"Yeah, it's you," she murmured softly. "Always there to dry my tears. That's why I love you so much." She went quiet for a moment, and he wondered if she was thinking about her dad's funeral. He'd been overseas at the time but had called in every favor he had to come home to be with her. She'd cried so hard that night, and he held her tight as her tears soaked through his shirt. They'd fallen asleep like that in her bed, and in the morning she'd told him how much she loved him.

She didn't need to add *like a brother*, it was simply implied in the platonic way she looked at him.

"I love you too," he said, deciding to keep *but* not *like a sister* to himself.

She sniffed and pulled at her sweater. It lifted slightly from her hips and he caught a glimpse of her lace panties. He nearly bit off his tongue. "I put on something really nice," she began. "Then I went into his room."

"And?" he asked, when all the while what he really wanted to do was put his fingers in his ears and scream "lalalalalala".

"He laughed, Matt." She shook her head, her hair brushing over her shoulders. "He laughed like it was some sort of big joke. Like it was some...some sort of birthday gag."

"You know Caleb's drunk, right?" He took a long, slow breath, trying to decide whether to hug or kill the guy.

"Yeah, I know, but still..." she said, then murmured something about a pork chop that he didn't understand.

"It's his thirtieth birthday, he drank a few beers. Laughing has nothing to do with you. Believe me. He probably thought we were messing with him." He gave her a wink and, wanting to lighten her mood, said, "He probably thought you were trying to distract him so I could put icing on his nose."

"You think?"

"Yeah. If he had been sober, and you walked in wearing, whatever it is you're wearing under that sweater, it would have opened his eyes."

"You think so?"

"I know so."

"I'm not so sure." There was a little quiver in her breath as she exhaled. "All I know is I'm never doing that again."

Halle-freaking-luiah!

They sat there for a very long time, listening to the waves lap against the shore and the nearby trees rustle as animals scurried in the woods around them. A boat went by and the dock swayed in the wake.

He looked at the sky, and pointed. "There's Venus." That pulled a small smile from her. When she was young, her dad was a big stargazer, which was how she'd come by her name. As kids, Sky was always pointing things out in the sky. They'd lie in the grass for hours and draw the images with their fingers. He chuckled inwardly, because every time she pointed out Venus, he always came back with, "Where's Uranus?"

"The third brightest object in the sky after the sun and moon," she said. "Also the Roman goddess of love and beauty."

Matt couldn't help but think her father should have named her Venus instead of Sky.

She looked around, pointed, then drew out another cluster of stars.

"Little Dipper," he said.

"Right."

They went quiet again, and Sky leaned into him. He put his arm around her and as he held her, he tried not to think about how good she felt in his arms. Fuck. He was so torn. He wanted her happy, but the thoughts of her and Caleb together burned a hole in his gut. Then again, he'd rather her be with Caleb than someone else, so he had better damn well get his shit together and figure out how to make that happen.

Sky finally broke the silence and said, "I think I'm going to have to take a different approach to get him to notice me."

"What are you talking about?" he asked.

"I have an idea."

She looked at him, and beneath the full moon, he caught the glint in her eyes. His stomach tightened, and even though he had no clue as to what she was thinking, something in his gut told him he wasn't going to like it.

"I once heard that a guy wants what another guy has."

He angled his head and pressed his thumb and index finger to his temples. Oh this was bad. This was so fucking bad. "What are you getting at?"

"I think the only way for me to get Caleb to take notice, is if I'm with another guy."

Okay, so now he had to see her with some *other* guy. As if watching her with Caleb wasn't enough. Who the fuck did he piss off in this world anyway? He was a good guy, played by the rules—mostly—and even cared for his Gran. He shook his head in disgust. Maybe nice guys really did finish last.

"You remember that movie we watched a long time ago. The romantic comedy starring Jennifer Aniston?"

"You've made me watch a lot of movies, Sky. I don't remember one from the other."

"It's the one where she wants her boss to notice her so she pretends she has a fiancé."

He searched his memory bank, but all the romantic comedies they'd watched over the last year were running together in his brain. "No, I don't really remember."

"What if Caleb saw me with another guy? Saw me laughing, having fun and getting cozy and intimate. Maybe then he'd look at me differently."

Shit, he really, really didn't like the sound of this. He grabbed a fistful of his hair and looked out over the water. "That won't work," he said soberly, turning back to her.

She blinked up at him, and when she trailed her tongue over her bottom lip, he wanted to kiss the hell out of her and show her what *would* work.

Cool it, Matt. She's not yours.

"Why not?" she asked.

"Caleb's not the kind of guy who would hone in on another man's territory. You and I both know that."

"I know. " She dipped her feet into the water and he

listened to the splashing sounds as she wiggled her toes. "But in the movie they planned a mutual breakup. I could do that."

"You've given this a lot of thought, haven't you?"

She nodded and patted the deck. "I've been sitting here for a while."

"Okay so what happens after this mutual breakup?"

"Once Caleb knows I'm free, we could get together."

Holy Christ, this was laughable. Except he wasn't laughing. He exhaled slowly. This had to be the worst idea he'd ever heard. "Didn't it backfire in the movie?"

She arched a brow. "So you do remember?"

"Vaguely," he said, even though it wasn't true. But he'd seen enough romantic comedies over the years to know how they played out. Besides that, he knew a bad idea when he heard it. "I don't know, Sky."

"I think it's exactly what I need to do to open Caleb's eyes."

He pushed his feelings for her aside for a moment and gave it serious consideration. Maybe seeing her with another guy, getting cozy and intimate, was just the thing Caleb needed to snap some sense into him and see how great of a girl she was. And the truth was, he wanted her happy, and he knew Caleb was a good guy. Better her with him then some random asshole who might not treat her properly.

"Okay fine, so maybe it will work," he said. "There's only one problem with this whole plan."

"What?"

"Where are you going to find a guy on such short notice and get him to pretend to be in love with you?"

"I think I'm looking at him."

5

Before she could say another word, Matt jumped to his feet and started pacing the length of the dock. He reached the end in three long strides then started back her way.

"No way. No way, Sky," he ranted as he passed by her. "You can't ask me to do that. It won't work."

Sky reached out and grabbed Matt's arm, desperate to stop him, to make him understand. He pulled away from her, pounding his left hand into his right palm and mumbling curses under his breath.

"Just for the weekend, Matt. Come on. You know I'd do it for you." It was true, they always had each other's backs and she'd do anything in the world for him. They both knew that.

He stopped mid-stride and faced her. "Sky, you can't be serious. This is crazy."

"It's not *that* crazy," she said quickly. "Who better than to open Caleb's eyes than his best friend?" She moved closer to him. "You two are tight. You can talk about me, get him to look, to notice." She put her hand on his chest. His skin felt warm despite the cold lake water. His strong heart pounded hard against her hand. "I think *you* of all people can open his eyes."

His hand closed over hers, big, strong and protective. He went quiet for a long moment, then he finally said, "You really want me to do this?"

She caught the tortured look on his face and felt a moment of guilt. Maybe she was asking too much of him. "Yes, but if you really, really don't want to, I can try to find someone else to—"

A low groan sounded in his throat, cutting her off. "You are not asking anyone else," he said through gritted teeth.

"Does that mean—"

"Yes, it means I'll do it." His nostrils flared as he sucked in a breath. "I'll do it, okay?"

"You will?"

"Yes."

Of course she couldn't ask for so much without giving him something in return. "I tell you what, in return for helping me, I'll book four weekends off in a row like you've been trying to get me to do, and help you study."

"No," he said.

Her stomach dropped, worried that he was suddenly having second thoughts. "No. You won't do it?"

"Of course I'll do it. But I want you to do something else for me in exchange."

She angled her head, her curiosity piqued. "Oh, and what might that be?"

"I want you to book the weekends off, but instead of helping me study, I want you to write."

Her head came back with a start. She hadn't talked about her writing in ages and was shocked that Matt had actually brought it up. Publishing a book was a dream, maybe even a foolish one. Reality was her working in her dad's bar and paying the bills.

"You want me to write?"

"Yeah."

"I...why?"

He cupped her chin, and the smile he gave her was so warm, soft and caring, it made her feel a little weak in the knees. "It's your dream isn't it?"

Her throat felt a little tight, making it difficult to say, "Yes, but—"

"No buts. It's the only way I'll help you."

Surprised by his condition, and a little touched that he'd never forgotten her lost dream, she nodded. "Okay, you have a deal. Tomorrow we'll start acting different around each other. We'll take it slow, so it's believable to our friends. Although Kat and Tallulah will know what we're up to. This kind of was Kat's idea."

He shook his head. "Now why doesn't that surprise me."

"She was the one who helped get Tallulah and Garrett together."

"I know. I was there at the wedding when it all happened, remember?"

"Right." The wedding she'd missed.

"So what exactly do you want me to do?" he asked.

"Pretend like you're suddenly seeing me differently I guess."

He scrubbed his chin, the rasp of his stubble carrying in the calm night. She focused on his big hands, and once again thought about Matt and kink. Damn you, Kat!

"How do I go about doing that, Sky?"

"You know, touch me a lot."

"You want me to touch you?"

"Yeah."

He put his hand on her shoulder and brushed his thumb over her cheek. The rough pad feeling oddly erotic as it skidded over her skin. "Like this?"

"Yeah," she croaked out, hyper-aware of the shiver moving through her.

"What else?"

"Just stay close I guess." Honestly, she really wasn't sure what they'd have to do. No guy had ever fallen for her before so she had nothing to draw on except the movies she'd watched. "We should laugh a lot and make it look like we're having fun together."

"But we always laugh and have fun together," he said, his voice sounding a bit deeper than it had seconds ago.

"Then I don't know. I guess we'll just have to wing it and try to make it believable."

"Jack's a hard guy to fool."

"Then you'd better brush up on your acting skills and start looking at me like you see me as more than the pigtailed girl on the playground."

He dipped his head, his eyes moving over her face, a slow, careful perusal that she felt all the way to her core. Why was it suddenly harder to fill her lungs?

"Yeah, like that," she said, feeling a little breathless.

She sucked in air. Honestly, he was either a quick study, or... A burst of unease moved through her as Kat's words ripped through her thoughts.

Matt. He likes you.

Kat had to be wrong. She just had to be. Matt wouldn't be helping her if *he* liked her.

He wet his lips and his mouth was so close to hers, for a minute she thought he was going to kiss her. "Normally I take the lead with a woman, but I think in this case you better call the shots. I don't how far you want me to go."

"O...okay," she said, realizing she was glimpsing another side of Matt. A dominant side. A side he probably reserved for the bedroom. Her body trembled almost uncontrollably as her thoughts careened in an erotic direction. Unnerved by the things racing through her brain, she quickly shook her head to get it on straight. What the hell was going on with her, and why did she suddenly find the idea of kink so exciting? Was it possible she had deep dark desires that she never knew about? Or perhaps it was just because she hadn't had sex in a long time. Yeah, that had to be it.

"Are you cold?" he asked, brushing his hands up and down her arms to create friction with heat.

"A bit," she lied. She wiped a bead of perspiration from her forehead and stepped back from his hold. "I guess I'll see you in the morning then."

His gaze shifted to her mouth. "Sure."

She paused and looked at him standing there on the dock, the moonlight spilling over his half-naked body. "Are you sure you're okay doing this?" she asked, suddenly not so certain about this half-cocked plan she'd talked him into. "I mean—"

"I'll do whatever it takes to get you what you want, Sky."

Her heart squeezed, because Matt really was one of the good guys. "Thanks," she said and turned to go. Leaving him standing on the dock, she hurried back to the cottage. She slipped into bed beside Kat, and Kat stirred but didn't wake. For that she was grateful, because she didn't want to explain why she was in bed with her and not Caleb.

She closed her eyes, willing sleep to come, but her thoughts went to Matt and his condition on him helping her. It really did warm her all over to find out he'd never forgotten her dreams, and no matter what he said, she vowed to help him study, because she wanted to help him fulfill his dreams too. She looked at the woman asleep beside her. Maybe Kat was right. Maybe Matt was the whole package. Sky rolled onto her side, hoping one day Matt would find the girl of his dreams. If he did, she'd do whatever it took to help him get what he wanted.

With that last thought in mind, Sky dozed off, and when

she woke to the morning sun streaming in through the crack in the curtains, she found a sleepy Kat staring at her.

"Good morning," Sky said.

Kat frowned. "I'm guessing it's not that good. Otherwise you wouldn't be here with me."

Sky groaned and put her arm over her head, knowing Kat wouldn't let her out of that room without explaining. "You're right. Last night didn't go down quite like I'd hoped."

"Aww, I'm sorry, honey." Kat pulled Sky's arm away from her face. "Are you okay?"

She nodded as her friend looked at her with sympathetic eyes. "I will be as long as Caleb doesn't remember laughing at my seduction."

Kat adjusted her pillow against the headboard and sat up. "He did have a lot to drink."

"Yeah, that's what Matt said."

"Matt?"

"I ran into him at the dock last night. He said Caleb only laughed because he was drinking and probably thought it was a joke."

"What else did he say?"

She looked at Kat, and a mixture of excitement and nervousness bubbled up inside her. She opened her mouth and found herself spilling the details. "That he'd help me open Caleb's eyes."

"Oh? Do tell."

"Remember what you were saying about a man wanting what another man has?"

Kat sat up straighter. "Are you serious? Matt's agreed to be the other guy, to help you snag Caleb."

"Yeah."

"Wow, he's one hell of a friend, Sky. He must really like you."

She nodded quickly. "He said he'd do whatever it takes."

Kat regarded her with wide, all-knowing eyes. "I just bet he will."

"What's that supposed to mean?"

"What it means is that you're going to have to really pour it on thick to convince Caleb."

Sky puckered her lips. "You think?"

"I know."

"So what are you suggesting? How thick do you think we'll have to pour it on?" she asked, curious to learn from her vivacious, bold friend who knew a hell of a lot more about relationships and men than she did.

Kat shuffled on the bed, like she was totally excited by the idea of her and Matt pretending to be an item. "You'll have to pour it on *all the way*, my friend."

Her stomach tightened. "All the way?" she repeated, not really liking the gleam in Kat's eye or the way she said *all the way*, because to Sky *all the way* meant sex.

"Yeah, lots and lots of touching," Kat explained.

She relaxed a bit. "Yeah, I mentioned that to him."

"And don't forget the kissing."

"You think we have to kiss?"

"Sure. Couples who are crazy about each other, and especially ones in a new relationship, kiss all the time. You saw Luke and Emery last night, didn't you? Those two couldn't keep their hands off each other."

"Yeah but if we go from zero to hundred overnight, don't you think that's going to be a bit unbelievable? I told Matt we needed to take it slow."

"There's no time for slow, Sky." She clapped her hands together, three quick rhythmic slaps. "This is the twenty-first century. Everything happens fast these days."

"Don't you think it will shock everyone? Make them wonder what's really going on? Matt and I have been best friends forever, if all of a sudden we start kissing—"

"Oh, don't worry," Kat said, a knowing smirk on her face. "I'm pretty sure it won't shock anyone."

"What's that supposed to mean?"

"Nothing." Kat bit her bottom lip and gave Sky a look that said she knew something Sky didn't. Sky eyed her friend and was about to push when Kat said, "I just think there should be lots and lots of kissing."

She'd kissed Matt before, of course. On the cheek. Like a brother. Although there was that one time when they all played spin the bottle. She'd kissed him on the lips then, but they were two clumsy tweens who didn't know what they were doing.

"I don't know, Kat."

"Well, I do, and if you want to make this work, you should listen to me. Don't worry, it will be fun."

"Fun?"

"Sure, even if it is pretend, you're in for a good time." Kat grabbed one of the throw pillows and pulled it to her chest for a hug. "Because I can tell he's a great kisser." She looked at the ceiling and briefly closed her eyes. "And if you have to kiss someone, and make it really convincing, then you definitely want a guy who knows what he's doing. Matt was the best choice for this little ruse."

Sky ran her tongue over her bottom lip. She'd have to kiss Matt? She felt a quick flash of panic. "I don't know, Kat. I still think this is taking things too far too fast."

"You do want Caleb, right?"

"Yeah." Her thoughts traveled to the man in the room next to theirs. She was pretty confident he wouldn't remember her botched seduction when he woke up. If he did, Matt would no doubt jump in and play it off as a joke. He was good at coming to her rescue.

"Then it's no holds barred. I mean come on, Sky, the man calls you Skywalker. Short of a good swift kick to the balls to get his attention, you'll have to really throw herself into your role with Matt."

She bit her bottom lip. "Maybe I'm making a mistake. Maybe I should call this whole thing off."

"Don't even think about it. This plan is brilliant actually." Kat nodded thoughtfully. "Oh yeah, once you and Matt start touching, kissing and sneaking off to bed like lovers, it's going to open a lot of eyes."

"You think so?"

"Uh huh." Kat's head continued to bob, and she curled a long strand of her hair around her index finger as she went quiet for a moment, like she was lost in her own thoughts. Sky took that time to think about this plan, what Kat was suggesting.

"Wait!" Sky sat up and shimmied backward to rest against the headboard. "What did you mean by sneaking off to bed like lovers?"

"Once you start kissing in front of everyone, they're going to expect you two to share a room. Like I said, things happen fast these days, and we *are* all adults, you know. And adults do adult things."

She took a moment to entertain the idea of sneaking off to bed with Matt. The sound of Tallulah and Garrett entering the cottage snapped her back to the moment. What the hell was she doing? "I'm not going to do...*that*."

"I'm not saying you have to do anything behind closed doors. Unless of course you want to." Kat studied her carefully, like she was gauging her reaction. "I really hope you want to though. Then I can live vicariously through you." She squirmed beside her, clearly excited by the prospect of Sky sleeping with Matt. "You can tell me how awesome he is, how his hands feel on your body...slapping your ass."

Oh gawd.

Sky's mind took that moment to conjure up images of her

and Matt in bed. Despite her best efforts to push them away, she visualized herself up on her knees, Matt behind her doing naughty, delicious...*kinky* things with his hands. A small wheezing sound escaped her throat and she started fussing with the bedding to pretend all this salacious talk wasn't getting to her. She was a vanilla girl and it was crazy to think how much this all intrigued her.

She shook her head to clear it, and all dirty thoughts came to a screeching halt. Okay, she was definitely getting in over her head here. Maybe this was a stupid plan that would blow up in her face.

"I don't think—"

"Sky," Kat started, cutting her off with a huff. "If you want him, you have to do whatever it takes. Even if that means kissing and touching Matt intimately."

"Okay, kissing and touching I can handle. But I'm not doing anything behind closed doors. It doesn't ever have to come to that."

Sky caught the mischievous gleam backlighting Kat's green eyes. "Of course it doesn't."

"Oh, I get it." She laughed and playfully whacked her friend. "You were just messing with me. You had me worried for a minute there."

Kat arched a brow. "Worried? I'm not so sure it was worry I saw in your eyes."

"You did. Matt and I are friends. Nothing more," she assured Kat.

"Whatever you say."

"I told you. He doesn't like me like that."

Kat slid from the bed and stretched. "So you've said."

"If he did, he wouldn't go through with the plan. He thinks Caleb and I would be great together. He said it a few times now. He wants us together."

"I'm not arguing with you, Sky. I get it. You're friends."

Kat blew a wispy strand of hair from her forehead, but there was a gleam when she turned back to Sky and added, "I'm just not sure who you're trying to convince here. Me or you."

"I'm trying to convince you, of course." She and Matt were friends. Of that she was certain. Even if she did have to start touching and kissing him, it didn't mean anything. And she wasn't going to give another second thought to sleeping with him, or how naughty he was behind closed doors.

She didn't think.

——————

Matt rolled onto his side. After a sleepless night, he prayed come the light of day Sky would see the folly behind her plan. Otherwise he'd have to go through with touching her and... God knows what else. He was pretty damn certain stepping on an IED would be less painful.

The boat swayed against the dock and he could hear laughing coming from the cottage. He stole a glance at his watch and guessed everyone was up and getting ready to plan the day. He kicked his sheet off and glanced down to see little Matt—or rather *big* Matt at this time of the morning—standing at half-mast. Shit. What the hell was going to happen when Sky started playing up to him? How the hell would he be able to keep his feelings for her hidden? He was like Pavlov's dog for Christ sakes. His dick was conditioned to rise to the occasion whenever Sky got close.

He jumped to his feet and ran his hands though his hair, finger-combing it in place. After a quick trip to the small bathroom, he made his way to the cottage. He stepped into the kitchen and looked over the counter to find everyone sitting around the living room drinking coffee and nibbling on last night's birthday cake. Emery and Luke were at the stove, flipping pancakes.

"Morning," he said to Luke and Emery when they turned to see him.

"Look what the cat dragged in," Luke said, slapping Matt on the shoulder.

"Fuck off," Matt said, then turned to Emery. Shit. He gave her a sheepish look. "Sorry." In an attempt to be one hundred percent opposite from his old man, Matt showed respect to women. He cringed thinking about the women that had come and gone from his father's life when Matt was young, and the disgusting display of foul language aimed their way after his father had found the bottom of his bottle.

"Such a gentleman," Emery said, and whacked Luke with the spatula. "You could take a lesson from him."

Luke grabbed her and pulled her to him, sliding his hands around her back to cup her ass as Kat stepped up to the coffee pot. "Oh, yeah, you didn't seem to mind my un-gentle-manly ways last night." He gave her a light tap on her back-side and she squealed, but from the gleam in her eyes Matt could tell it was from excitement, not pain. Her arms went around Luke's neck and the two started kissing.

"Get a room already," he mumbled as he met Jack's smirk from the other side of the cottage. There was no hiding anything from that guy. Which might actually be a good thing. At least that was one less person they'd have to convince. Although the breakup might be a little harder to explain, and that's when Matt would really have to start acting.

Kat handed him a mug of coffee, and he plunked himself down onto the sofa next to Caleb. Sky came from the bedroom. He could feel her eyes on him, and his heart started beating a little faster. Would she have changed her mind? Would a good night's sleep have helped her see how easily this plan could backfire? In the movies, the one playing the fake lover always ended up with the girl. He scoffed. Hell, maybe this wasn't such a bad idea. Oh, but it was, he quickly reminded himself. There was no way Sky was ever going to fall for him, and even if she did, he didn't want her to. She deserved better.

Hungover and looking like shit, Caleb groaned, pulling Matt's thoughts back. Matt put his hand on Caleb's head and gave a little shove. "Dumbass."

"Don't, man," Caleb said, closing one eye. He palmed both ears, like he was trying to stop the spinning. "Why the hell did you let me drink so much?"

"You only turn thirty once," Jack said.

Tallulah, who was sitting on Garrett's lap, pointed to his glass on the table. "Drink your orange juice. It will make you feel better."

"Death is the only thing that would make me feel better." As everyone laughed, Caleb reached for his juice and took a big swig. "I didn't do anything stupid, did I?"

"No, nothing," Sky said quickly and rested her elbows on the counter behind her as she leaned against it. She crossed her legs at the angle, looking to all the world relaxed and rested. But Matt knew her well enough to know there was a storm going on inside her.

A strange look came over Caleb's face. "Sky...wait...did...?"

"Don't worry about it, pal," Matt piped in. "I was the last one up with you and you didn't do anything stupid. Believe me if you did, I'd never let you live it down."

Caleb nodded and finished his juice. "That's true."

Matt looked at Sky, and she gave him a grateful look when their eyes met. His glance dropped from her face to take in the knit cover-up she was wearing over her bikini, one that did little to hide her gorgeous curves. Damn, she looked so good. Then again, it didn't matter what she wore. She always looked good.

"Anyone need more coffee?" Kat asked from the kitchen

and when Matt shifted his focus to her, she dipped her finger into the icing and slowly licked it off. "Mmm, good." She lifted her plate and held it out to Sky. "Want some?" Sky scooped off a bit of the icing, put her finger into her mouth and sucked it clean. A soft, sexy bedroom moan sounded in her throat.

"Delicious," Sky said, going back for seconds.

Matt looked away. No way in hell could he watch her do that again, not without thinking about how much he'd like to smear that blue icing on her body and lick it off, slowly, carefully, until she was writhing beneath him and screaming out his name.

"What's everyone doing today?" Tallulah asked, and Matt could have kissed her, grateful for the distraction.

Kat pointed to the backyard. "I don't know about the rest of you, but I'm hitting that hammock and reading." She winked at Sky. "I got a hot new Jan Meredith book in my hands and can't wait to see what *her* sexy doctor is up to next."

"What?" Caleb said. He'd obviously heard something about a doctor but missed Kat's insinuation.

"Go back to sleep," Jack said, laughing. Caleb groaned and returned his attention to his juice.

"I think I'll join you out back," Tallulah said to Kat.

Matt kept glancing at Sky, waiting for some sign that she still wanted to go through with this. If only she'd get her attention off that frigging icing and onto him. She finally turned and glanced around the room.

"What are you boys up to?" she asked.

Jack put his legs up on the coffee table and glanced at Caleb. "Are we still taking the boat out?"

"Yeah, sure," Caleb said. "'Cause my head isn't spinning enough."

"Maybe I'll go fishing with you guys then?" Sky said.

All eyes turned to her. Matt pushed back in his seat, sinking into the cushions. All righty, then. Apparently the plan was a go.

"Since when do you like fishing?" Caleb asked.

With a casual shrug, she walked over to Matt and planted herself on the edge of the sofa beside him. He handed her his coffee. She took a swig, and while there was nothing out of the ordinary in what they were doing, he could feel the shift in the room.

She handed him back the mug and he placed it on the coffee table and pulled her onto his lap. Caleb stretched out, but didn't seem to notice anything unusual in in the way they were acting. Then again, why would he? Sky often plunked herself down on his lap, and sharing drinks between them was the norm. Which made Matt realize they'd have to go pretty far to convince their friend there was more to their relationship.

Sky fell onto him, sinking back into the sofa with him, and as she settled herself onto his lap, Matt's throat tightened. Jesus Christ, she felt good. Too fucking good. Her legs brushed over his, soft, warm and silky. She flicked her hair back and when he caught the sweet scent of her skin, he drew it deep into his lungs. The gentleman in him urged him to ignore the way his cock was thickening. But the man in him decided manners were overrated, taking his mind down a path he had no business going. Not anymore, anyway. And certainly not with her. She squirmed and he fisted his fingers, resisting the urge to scoop her up in his arms and haul her ass into the bedroom—along with the half-eaten cake.

"Matt said he'd help me reel in a big one," Sky said.

Oh yeah, I have a big one for you all right.

She wiggled slightly and her sweet ass pressed against his cock. Okay, this was torture, pure fucking torture, and if he didn't put a stop to it and get the hell out of there, there was no way anyone could hold him accountable for his actions. Just when he was about to climb to his feet and go for a good long swim, she ran her fingers through his hair, mussing it up.

"Isn't that right, Matt? You're going to help me reel in a big one?"

He cleared his throat. "Yeah. Right. Big. One." Awesome, now he was down to one-syllable words.

"Fine," Caleb said, one eye still closed as he cast a warning glace her way. "But no screaming like you did the last time we went fishing. My head can't handle that."

"I was twelve, Caleb," she shot back. "In case you haven't noticed, I'm all grown up now."

Matt shook his head at Caleb. What a dumbass. He had to be the only living, breathing male on the face of the earth who hadn't noticed Sky was all woman.

"Doesn't mean a thing." Caleb pulled her from Matt's lap and onto his. She yelped when he put her in a headlock and started rubbing his knuckles into her hair, then he stopped abruptly. "Wait...Sky?"

"Breakfast ready?" Matt jumped to his feet, redirecting everyone's focus.

"Come and get it," Emery said from the kitchen.

He grabbed Sky by the waist and lifted her from Caleb's lap and they exchanged a long, knowing look. Relief danced in her eyes as she wrapped her arm in his and dashed to the kitchen for breakfast. They ate their pancakes outside at the picnic table and when the dishes were cleared, the girls disappeared inside to prepare for a day of sunbathing.

"You sure you want to come?" Matt asked Sky.

She looked hesitant for a moment. "So far everyone seems to be noticing but Caleb."

"Yeah, I know."

She frowned and went quiet. Was it possible that she was having second thoughts? Giving her an out, he opened his mouth, about to call the whole thing off, until she blinked up at him with those beautiful dark eyes. His heart squeezed. When she looked at him like that, all he wanted to do was give her the moon and the stars, and everything she'd ever wanted. Which, of course, was Caleb. He chewed on that for a moment, then felt something in him give. Honest to God he had to be some sort of masochist, because if Caleb was who she wanted then Caleb was who she deserved to have and he'd damn well do whatever it took to help her get him and make her happy.

"Don't worry, by the end of the day, he'll see things differently." He was about to push her hair from her face, like he did any other day, then drew his hand back. The only touching they'd do from here on out was when they had an audience. "I promise, okay?"

The smile that spread across her plump lips was like a damn sucker punch. But it was nothing compared to what she did next. Going up on her toes, she put her arms around his shoulders and pressed her lips to his cheek. "You're the best friend a girl could ever have," she whispered, her warm breath rushing over his skin like a hot caress.

She went back on her heels and he made a fist and nudged her chin. "Yeah, that's me. Your best friend." Desperate to get away from her, he grabbed his T-shirt and pulled it off. "I'm going to take a quick swim before we go." He started toward the dock and in usual Sky fashion she ran after him and jumped on his back for a piggyback ride. Holy hell, he could feel the heat between her legs pressing into his back. And knowing nothing but a skimpy pair of bikini bottoms separated their bodies was just about more than he could take at the moment.

He took off running and she tried to break free, but he held her tight. His shirt slipped from his hands, and he jumped into the water with her still on his back. He let her go when they hit bottom and she pushed away from him. They both came up sputtering.

"Matt," she screamed. "You're a dead man."

Tell me something I don't know.

She splashed water in his face, then grabbed his shoulders. She pushed herself out of the water and tried to dunk him under. Her hard nipples scraped over his chest, then all of a sudden they were right there, directly in front of his mouth. All he had to do was flick his tongue out to brush them through the thin piece of fabric separating her hard nubs from his mouth—if he wanted to. And yeah he wanted to. She wrapped her legs around his waist to hold on. Shit. If she slid downward she was going to feel his hard cock. He wrapped his arms around her waist to hold her in place, then dragged her under again. She kicked off him and swam back to the dock, while he went deeper.

He surfaced a few feet out and spotted Jack watching them.

"You don't play fair," she said and grabbed his T-shirt. His look was coy when she said, "But neither do I." She wiped her face with his shirt, then dried the rest of her body. Great. Now her scent would be impregnated in the fabric and he'd have to smell her all fucking day.

"I'll get into some dry clothes and meet you back here," she called out and took off toward the cottage.

Matt stayed in the water until his hard-on receded, then he climbed out and sat on the dock beside Jack.

"So what's going on?" Jack asked.

Matt shrugged. "Don't know what you're talking about."

"I guess I always knew you liked Sky. Hell we all did. But I just never thought you were going to do anything about it."

He wasn't going to. At least not until after he became a doctor and was worthy of her. "Things changed."

"When?"

"Doesn't matter."

"I guess it doesn't." He patted Matt on the shoulder. "I'm just glad you finally went for it."

"Why do you say that?"

"You two are good together, Matt. I've always thought that."

They might have fun together but that didn't mean that he was right for her. Not wanting to talk about Sky anymore, he turned the subject back to a common ground. "I hear Theo's strong enough to get back to work." He thought about their fellow comrade who'd recently been discharged, and the shrapnel he'd taken in the leg. "He's been working with Kat at the hospital and making great progress."

"I offered him a job at the bike shop, but Luke is expanding his security business and I think he's going try that for a bit."

Beside them the boat started and Matt climbed to his feet. "Looks like Caleb is ready." He grabbed his wet shirt and pulled it on, then jumped onto the deck. Jack followed him and Garrett came running from the cottage with all the fishing gear.

Matt looked past his shoulders to see Sky coming behind him. Dressed in a pair of cut-off shorts and a tank top that showed her curves, she looked as beautiful as ever. Her hair was wet, drying in the warm morning sun. He held his hand out to her when she reached the boat and pulled her on board just as the boat rocked. Her body collided with his and she wrapped her arms around him to hold on.

"Whoa, you okay?"

"Yeah," she said, sounding a bit breathless.

Garrett and Jack started preparing their rods as Caleb motored the cruiser out to the middle of the huge lake. Sky gripped the metal bar running along the sides to hang on. She leaned over slightly to look into the water, that cute little ass of hers in the air. Matt pressed against her, and put his hands on the rails on either side of hers.

Yeah, okay, he was definitely a masochist.

The boat swayed in the light waves and after setting the anchor, Caleb reached for his rod. "Skywalker," he called out. "Get over here and I'll show you how to catch a big one. Only thing our boy Matt here can catch is a cold."

Matt pushed away from her, and she maneuvered around Jack and Garrett to sit beside Caleb. Matt grabbed his own rod and put on his lure. He casted it over the side and listened to Caleb give Sky directions. He clenched down hard on his jaw and worked not to go batshit crazy as Caleb and Sky laughed. Fighting the possessive tug on his emotions, he reminded himself he'd have to get used to seeing them together, because this was what Sky wanted. Another thought hit and his stomach tightened with unease. When those two got together, he'd no doubt see less and less of them. Sure, they'd invite him along, but what would that make him—the third wheel? Shit, he wanted this for her, but other than Gran, Sky and Caleb were the only family he had. It would destroy him if he lost either one from his life.

Commanding himself to think about something else, he cast his rod from the opposite side of the boat and glanced out over the water. Two girls sped by on a jet ski and waved. He recognized them. They vacationed at a cottage just down the road. They jogged by Caleb's place often, and a couple weeks ago had joined the guys for a drink. Maybe tomorrow he'd go for a run with them and see where it led. Maybe that would help him forget about the long, lonely nights he'd have ahead of him. Before he could give the idea any more consideration, his bobber dipped below the surface and he tightened his hold on his reel. A few minutes later he pulled in a speckled trout. After catching the first fish of the day, the rest of the morning and early afternoon passed quickly and everyone except Caleb and Sky had caught their share of fish.

"I'm starved," Caleb said, rubbing his stomach. "We should head back."

"Yeah, and maybe we can cook up that 'big' one you and Sky caught," Garrett ribbed.

"Ha ha, funny guy," Caleb shot back.

"Guess you should have stuck with Matt," Jack said to Sky when Matt pulled the anchor and Caleb started the boat to take them all back to shore. When they reached the dock, Sky jumped from the boat, signaling for Matt to follow. Matt walked with her up to the cottage, and when they were out of earshot, she stopped and turned to him.

She crinkled her nose and pushed her hair from her face, only for it to fall back into place. "I don't think that went so well."

Matt looked over his left shoulder to watch Caleb tie the boat up while the other two gathered up the gear. "Our plan kind of got off track when he called you over."

"I know, I didn't have a chance to play up to you, and all Caleb did was treat me like one of the guys."

Unable to help himself, he tucked her hair behind her ear. His fingers brushed her cheeks and his entire body went on fire. Even though he knew it wasn't in his best interest he said, "I guess there is only one thing we can do."

"What's that?

"Hit him over the head with it."

Before he could think better of it, he slid his hand around her neck and drew her mouth to his, working to convince himself he was doing this for Sky. But the second his lips touched hers, he knew the real truth. He *needed* to taste her, and the ruse was nothing but a damn excuse to finally feel her mouth moving under his.

She opened for him and a moan that didn't have to be

faked crawled out of his throat. Her warm fingers slid around his back and when she pressed against him, he fisted her hair and deepened the kiss. His tongue slipped inside and when he tasted her sweetness, his cock swelled inside his shorts.

Her hands gripped his shirt, and desire to haul her off to bed twisted inside him. She made a soft, mewling sound that set off a storm inside him. Completely rattled by the things she made him feel, moisture broke out on his forehead. He breathed deep. The rich scent of her skin singed his blood. He should stop. He needed to stop. But as she kissed him back, his mind abandoned any rational thought. All he could think about was the erection tenting his pants and how much he wanted to get her out of her clothes so he could kiss her all over...drive inside her.

"Get a room," Jack said as he walked past them, his voice bringing Matt's attention back around.

Matt broke the kiss and inched back. He rocked on his feet, working to catch his breath. He took in the warm flush on Sky's face, the pucker in her well-kissed lips, the upward tilt of her head as she stood there with her eyes still closed, her mouth poised open.

"Sky," he whispered, barely able to squeeze that one word out as his cock raged for more.

Her lids flicked open and she glanced around, like she was trying to orient herself. "What?" she asked.

He gestured toward Caleb, who was staring at them from the dock, shock all over his face. "I think it worked."

6

"**M**att?"

In the boat's dark sleeping quarters, Matt rolled on the mattress to face her.

"Yeah?" he whispered, his voice sounding a bit hoarse.

Sky pushed off the bottom step and moved closer to his bed. "You awake?"

"I am now."

She listened to the sound of him rubbing his hands through his hair as she plunked herself on the edge of the mattress next to him. The warm, earthy scent of his skin reached her nose.

"You okay?" he asked.

She nodded, even though he likely couldn't see it. "Kat kicked me out."

He rustled around and flicked on the small lamp on the wall near the head of the bed. They both blinked against the brightness. "What are you talking about?"

"She said in order to make this really believable, I'd have to spend the night here with you. I flat-out refused, but then she started coughing. She told me she was coming down with a cold, and that I was welcome to share the bed with her if I wanted to catch it. I'm pretty sure she was lying."

He went up on one elbow and the single sheet covering him fell to his waist. Her gaze dropped to his naked chest and lingered there. Oh my. When had he gotten so buff? Her fingers went to her lips, which still tingled from the kiss he'd given her earlier that day. When her glance went back to his face, she wondered if he knew she was checking him out.

"You can take the bed," he said and started to climb out.

She put her hand on his chest to stop him, but almost lost focus when her fingers met with packed muscle and a strong heartbeat. "No. I'll sleep in the chair. I just wanted to let you know I was here."

That earned her a scowl. "You're not taking the chair."

"You're not taking it either," she countered.

"Then come here."

Before she realized what he was doing, he had his arm around her and hauled her into bed beside him. "It's not like we haven't slept in the same bed together before," he grouched, still sounding half-asleep.

"That's true," she murmured as the warmth of his body enveloped her.

He grabbed the blankets and pulled them over her, then switched off the light. "Then get some sleep," he mumbled and turned his back to her.

She settled in next to him, her back pressed against his. Curling up tighter, she listened to his soft breathing but couldn't quiet her mind down enough to sleep. After the heated kiss that totally took her by surprise—and oh what a kiss it was—everyone went on with their day as usual. She joined the girls for a little sunbathing, while the guys kicked back and relaxed on the dock. After dinner, but before the bonfire, she'd caught Matt and Caleb talking privately and was dying to know what was said. She did however notice the curious glances Caleb kept casting her way.

"Matt?"

"Hmm."

"What did you say to Caleb?"

A beat of silence and then, "I told him I was interested in you."

"What did he say?"

"It really threw him at first."

"And then?"

"And then I told him to take a good look at you."

"I did notice him looking."

Matt shifted on the mattress and she turned to face him. With her eyes adjusted to the dark, she took in his profile as he stared at the ceiling, his hands behind his head. "Yeah, he was looking all right."

A little bubble of excitement welled up inside her. "I told you this would work."

He went quiet for a moment, then, like he'd done when they shared a bed before, pulled her onto his chest. "You were right. Now let's get some sleep."

His hand fell from her shoulder to stroke a tender caress over her arm, and she wondered if he even realized he was doing it. Regardless, *she* knew, and suddenly so did her body. Warm shivers traveled all the way to her toes, and when she quivered, he adjusted the blankets over her and pulled her in tighter.

She settled in next to him and breathed in the scent of his skin as she listened to his strong heartbeat. Soon sleep pulled at her and when she woke, she found herself in the exact same position. She tilted her head to find Matt looking at her.

"Morning," she said, then stretched out. "You been awake long?"

"Not long."

The sound of the others packing up reached her ears. "I guess everyone is getting ready to head back."

"Yeah, Caleb needs to get back early, and I really need to hit the books."

"I work a shift tonight too." She slipped from the bed and Matt stood up behind her. He brushed up against her in the small quarters, and she felt something push into the small of her back. Wait, that wasn't...was it?

She was about to turn and check, but he darted into the bathroom. Shrugging it off as nothing more than a guy's early-morning erection, she smoothed her hair back and adjusted her shorts and T-shirt, which still smelled like smoke from the fire last night. After Matt came from the bathroom, she slipped in behind him, and listened to him dig around in his duffle bag. She came out to find him dressed.

"All set?" he asked, giving her a whack on her ass to set her in motion. The feel of his hard palm on her soft backside went right through her, eliciting a shudder and sending her thoughts in an erotic direction. She blew her hair from her face and bit back a breathy moan as she pictured Matt's hard body on top of hers, doing delicious, naughty things with his hands. She gulped. Why the hell was she suddenly thinking about sex—and with Matt? It was a friendly tap, not a sexual one, and he'd slapped her ass numerous times before. Never had she conjured up such naughty images because of it. She was sure Kat was to blame for all this. Planting naughty ideas in her mind, then offering her a lick of icing to make them bloom.

"Move it," he said, giving her another slap.

She hurried off the boat and Matt followed her. The others were all busy packing up, paying little attention to them this morning. She'd heard the guys ribbing Matt last night after their kiss, but other than that, nothing. Kat was right. No one seemed that shocked. Well, with the exception of Caleb. The others were either too self absorbed in their own relationships, or had, on some level, expected a relationship to eventually happen between her and Matt. Probably because they were always together and her friends were working under the assumptions that guys and girls couldn't just be friends without something...*happening*.

After gathering her gear and packing her car, she drove back to the city with Kat. Tallulah went with her husband in his vehicle. Kat grilled her the whole way home, but Sky had nothing to spill. She simply slept in the same bed as Matt. Honestly, she was not going to have sex with him, no matter how desperate Kat was to live vicariously through her.

She dropped Kat off at her place, which was the apartment building across the street from hers, and parked her car in her assigned spot, next to Matt's motorcycle. She dashed inside to get changed. She climbed the three flights of stairs to her apartment. It wasn't a great place, and certainly not where she wanted to raise a family, but it would do in the interim, and Matt lived directly across the hall from her, which she loved. She stepped up to his door and knocked to see if he was there or had run to check on his Gran. When no answer came she hurried inside her place, took a quick shower, then headed to Sky Bar. She slipped in through the back door and found Matt behind the bar, filling a carafe of beer.

"What do you think you're doing?" Sky asked as she tucked her purse under the bar and grabbed her apron.

"Marco wanted to leave early. It's his kid's birthday, so I took over."

"You're not scheduled for tonight."

"No, but I didn't mind filling in until you got here. It's pretty quiet."

She pointed to his books on the counter. "Go. Study. I got this."

"Actually, I have to check on Gran." He pulled the cloth off his shoulder and draped it over hers. "I didn't get a chance to see her since I got back."

She shooed him away. "Okay, go."

He looked around the near-empty bar, and when she saw a flash of something in his eyes she followed his gaze to find Simon and three of his buddies all sitting around one table drinking. Simon was a hard character with a foul mouth. Single, mid-thirties, he usually came here on the weekends with his friends. He was a big guy, a poster boy for "all brawn and no brain". He liked to throw his weight around by picking fights, but the army guys who hung out at Sky Bar mostly ignored him.

"I'll be back before lock up."

"It's okay, go spend some time with Gran. I can lock up. I'll meet you at the apartment later."

Matt left through the back door and she brought the carafe over to Simon and his crew. "I take it this is for you."

"Yeah, put it on my tab, sweetheart," he said, his lecherous gaze sweeping the length of her.

She cringed inwardly, feeling the need for another shower, but tried not to show a reaction in front of them. "That tab is getting mighty long," she said with a smile.

The guys all laughed and she turned to go. She felt something brush against her backside, and sucked in a quick breath, ready to throw Simon out on his ass.

She turned back around, but the guys were ignoring her. Someone *had* touched her, of that she was sure, but with them all pretending otherwise, she had no idea who to call on it. Plus, getting into an altercation with these guys with no soldiers here to back her up probably wasn't wise.

"That will be the last one tonight, boys. I'm locking up early," she lied, wanting them out of there.

Walking back to the bar, she saw the kitchen staff out and poured herself a soda. Pulling out the small stool she kept behind the counter, she plunked herself down. She grabbed the notepad she kept in her apron, and thinking more about her agreement with Matt, and how he wanted her to write, she began jotting down notes. Soon enough she was lost in her own thoughts, and visions of Caleb as her hero in the story raced through her mind.

A tap on the bar top caught her attention and she stole a quick glance at her watch before her eyes met Simon's. Unease moved through her as she stood, noting that the bar was now empty, save for her and Simon.

"What can I do for you?" she asked.

"I want to pay my tab, sweetheart."

"Oh, okay." She grabbed her iPad and pulled up his bill. She printed it off and handed it to him. He pulled a stack of cash from his front pocket and started slapping the bills on the counter.

"So you say you're locking up early?"

"That's right. The place is empty. No need to keep it open." As soon as the words left her mouth, she tried to get them back, wishing she hadn't reminded him that it was just the two of them there.

He looked over his shoulder and wore a crooked grin when he turned back her way. "It is empty, isn't it?" The music on her dad's old jukebox changed, and a slow song came on.

"So how about a dance." Hand out palm up, he started around the bar toward her and she backed up.

"I don't dance with customers." She pointed in the opposite direction. "And it's time to go. Matt will be here in a second to lock up."

He momentarily stopped at the mention of Matt. "Fine then. Let's get out of here. Go somewhere where we can have some fun."

"That won't be happening." She backed up a few more inches and reached under the bar in search of the bat she kept there. One more step toward her and he'd be getting it over the head.

"Come on. I see the way you look at me."

"You must be mistaken." Her fingers closed over the wood and she shifted in her hands for a better grip. "I have a boyfriend and it's time for you to leave."

"Come on, baby. I'll show you a real good time. I bet I can make you moan louder than that bookworm of yours."

"Simon," she began, pulling the bat out and bracing it on her shoulder. She was about to take a good hard swing and hope for the best, but before she had the chance a voice sounded from behind Simon and stopped her cold.

"I believe the lady said it's time to leave."

Simon spun around to find Matt hovering close. Relief moved through her but it was short lived when Simon laughed. From the look on Matt's face, however, this was no laughing matter.

"Who's going to make me?" Simon said.

"I am."

Matt moved so fast, Simon had no time to react, and when the crack of bone reached her ears, she pulled her cell from her back pocket. As the two men dueled it out, the fight spilled into the lounge area, and she called Garrett.

A chair skidded across the room as Matt threw himself at Simon, sending him crashing onto one of the tables. He gripped Simon by the front of his shirt and repeatedly punched him in the face. Her stomach turned inside out and it occurred to her that she'd never seen Matt like this. A chorus of violent sounds as fists hit and bones crunched filled the air. Good God, if he didn't stop he was going to kill Simon. She was about to scream at him when he finally pulled back. Simon groaned and rolled off the tabletop, falling to the floor with a loud thud. As he lay there moaning, Matt rushed to her. Blue eyes full of worry searched hers as he framed her face with his hands.

He ran his thumbs over her cheeks and assessed her. Hands that were violent moments ago were now tender as they brushed her face. "Sky, are you okay?"

"I thought you were going to kill him," she whispered, her heart still pounding hard.

"I would have." He pressed his forehead to hers and sucked in a quick breath. "If he had hurt you, I would have, Sky."

She nodded and her voice came out a bit shaky when she tried to reassure him. "I'm fine. He didn't hurt me." Her hands shook as she placed the bat on the bar and, trying to lighten the mood, said, "Besides, I was ready with this."

"I'm so sorry," he rushed out, his response different than what she expected. He ran his hands through her hair, and drew her face to his chest, holding her so tight it was almost difficult to breathe. "I should have been here sooner. Actually, I never should have left you alone with him here. What was I thinking?"

"I told you to go, remember?" Even though she wasn't cold, she couldn't seem to keep her body from shaking. Okay, maybe the incident had frightened her more than she realized.

Matt cupped her face again and looked into her eyes. "He'll never step foot in this place again. You have my word on that."

"Okay," she croaked out.

"I need to call Garrett."

"I already did."

He gave her a smile. "That's my girl," he murmured. Simon continued to roll around on the floor as he held her. She stayed in his arms until sirens could be heard. Garrett and his partner came through the front door, and after speaking with Matt and Sky, he left, taking Simon with him.

Matt turned to her. "Let's get you home."

"Okay." She grabbed her purse, not about to protest and then noticed the cuts on his hands. "You're hurt."

He looked at his knuckles. "I'm okay."

"I have bandages at home."

Matt put his arm around her and walked her out the back door. The wind had picked up and clouds covered the night sky. A drop of cold rain hit her forehead and she shivered.

Matt quickened his steps. "We better hurry."

They turned the corner to walk the two blocks to their building but couldn't make it there before the skies opened up. The rain fell hard and they both took off running. Matt swiped his key and opened the building's front security door and they rushed inside. They hurried up the steps and when they reached their landing, Matt stood next to her, his back practically pressed against her chest.

For a second she wondered why he was following her into her place. They hung out often, for sure, but he was soaking wet and needed to get changed.

"Oh, right, your knuckles," she said as understanding dawned.

"I'm not leaving you alone tonight, Sky," he said, and something in his voice, something dark and protective, sent shivers skidding through her. "You're still shaking."

She opened her mouth to protest, after all she was a grown woman, but when she glanced over her shoulder to see him, the look in his eyes told her not to waste her breath.

"Open the door," he commanded and put his hand on it, fingers splayed.

She slipped her key in and turned the knob. Matt pushed it open and ushered her in. "I'll get those bandages," she murmured, her voice almost unrecognizable.

"Forget about the bandages." His gaze went from the top of her dripping hair to her wet shoes. "Go get into something dry." She took in the intense look on his face and wondered what the hell was going on with him—with her—as she darted to her room. Ever since they were kids Matt had been protective of those he cared about, but she'd never seen him in total alpha mode quite like this before. It was...different. But not in a bad way.

Pulling a pair of pajama pants from her dresser and a clean T-shirt that used to be Matt's until he shrank it in the wash, she walked back down the hall. The sound of a spoon clinking had her turning into her kitchen, and she found Matt standing over the kettle, pouring sugar into a teacup.

His wet shirt clung to him, showcasing broad shoulders and thick muscles. Her glance drifted downward, to jeans that hung low, but fit so nicely, especially around the ass area. A strange, strangled noise sounded in her throat, and there was nothing she could do to swallow it down. Matt turned to her.

"Hey."

"Hey yourself," she croaked out.

"I made you tea. Chamomile, no caffeine, a dash of sugar."

"Mmm, my favorite."

He poured the water into her cup, stirred it and handed it over.

She took a sip and said, "There's a beer in the fridge if you want it."

He pulled open the door, and, unable to help herself, she took another long look at his backside as he bent over. He'd always been well-built and strong, but how come she never noticed how... Her thoughts halted as she searched for the right word. Hot. Yeah, hot was the word. How come she never noticed how *hot* he was before?

"Drama or comedy?" he asked, closing the fridge, but she was far too slow to react.

"What?" Her gaze flew to his, and she could feel heat rushing to her face.

His brow furrowed and he angled his head. Shoot. Had he figured out that she was checking him out?

"Drama or comedy?" he asked again.

"Oh, comedy," she said. "I've had enough drama tonight."

His mood shifted so fast it caught her by surprise. He stepped up to her, his body close, and put his hand on the side of her head. Tender yet tough, his thumb stroked her cheek. His face tightened warily. "That will never happen again. I promise."

"Okay," she murmured for lack of anything else, and brought her teacup to her lips to hide the tremble. His gaze moved to her mouth and watched her drink. She hoped her hands didn't look as shaky as they felt as she tipped the cup and drank from it.

"Comedy it is," he said, walking past her. He grabbed the remote, flicked on the TV, then handed it to her. "Find us something. I'll be right back. I need to get changed."

"You don't have to stay," she said, even though the thought of him sleeping over gave her a great deal of comfort. Tonight had shaken her up more than she'd realized, but clearly Matt knew. He had been a medic in the army, and had dealt firsthand with shock and the aftereffects. Sky was safe with the security of their building, but knowing Matt was right here and not across the hall put her at ease.

With her feet tucked under her, she flicked through the channels until she came to a sitcom. Matt came back wearing clean jeans and a shirt. He sat down next to her and stretched out his legs.

Her glance moved over his face, taking in his hard profile as he took a pull from his bottle. He must have felt her staring because he turned to her and his face softened.

"How's Gran?" she asked.

"Not great." Worry lines bracketed his mouth. "She has a bad cold."

"Oh, sorry to hear that." Maybe a cold really was going around and Kat had caught it. "I'll have some chicken soup sent over from work."

He reached out and squeezed her hand. "Thanks, she'd probably like that." The TV blared in the background, and while Matt was staring at it, she could tell he wasn't really watching. He seemed to be lost in his own thoughts. His Gran had taken a fall not too long ago and he'd set her up with a medic alert alarm pendant. But that still didn't stop him from checking on her every day and doing a perimeter check of her house every night.

"You worry about her a lot, don't you?"

"Other than you and Caleb she's the only family I have." At the mention of Caleb he turned from her and went back to staring blankly at the TV, but she had the feeling something was wrong. She was about to ask when he said, "I don't like you working alone at night."

"I know, but I can't afford to hire out for every night shift."

"If you sold half the business to Marco, you'd be able to."

Realizing this was what had been on his mind, she held her hand up to stop him. "We've been through this, Matt."

"Marco loves the place. His investment will help with the bills and free up some of your time."

"It's my father's place. He trusted me with it."

"I know, but selling doesn't mean giving away what your father worked for. And don't you think he'd want you to follow your dreams?"

"Yeah, of course, but—"

"No buts. I just want you to think about it, okay? Promise me you'll at least do that."

She nodded. "Okay." They both turned toward the TV and she sipped her tea as her mind raced. Maybe Matt was right. The truth was, tonight scared her and as much as she loved her father and wanted to keep his bar going, she wanted more. How could she ever have a family if she was stuck behind the counter serving drinks most nights? How could she ever write the books she had in her head and heart? She mused over it a little longer.

Who was she kidding? With the current path she was on, she was never going to have the family and career she wanted. Then again, Caleb was beginning to notice her. But what if she sucked at being a writer?

"What if I never get published?" she asked over the rim of her teacup.

"Wouldn't it be worse if you never tried?"

She went quiet for a moment, because that was the same thing Kat had said to her about Caleb.

7

News of what happened at the bar with Simon spread quickly. Matt even received a text from Caleb to find out if he and Sky were okay. Now here it was, Friday night, a week since the incident and he was still hearing rumblings about it. At least that asshole and his friends knew better than to ever step foot in the place again. Regardless, for the next little bit he didn't plan to let Sky out of his sight.

Even though she'd protested when he insisted on staying with her that first night, he crashed on her sofa anyway because he knew the signs of shock when he saw it. He wanted to be there for her if she needed him.

Sky moved past him from the working side of the bar, pulling his attention. His heart squeezed as he looked at her. Over the course of the week, they'd spent almost every waking hour together, hanging out together at work, and even at home. Truthfully though, there was nothing unusual about that. They'd always spent as much time together as they could.

Over the course of the last week, when they weren't at

work and when he wasn't in front of his textbook and she wasn't writing on her laptop, they watched TV, and when nothing good was on, they'd go for a walk and he'd give her a piggyback ride as they stargazed. When they weren't around their friends, they had no need to put on a show, but that didn't stop them from touching, carrying on and sharing drinks like they always did—like real couples did. He'd slept on her couch every night, but it wasn't just because he wanted to watch over her and protect her from Simon, or let their friends believe they were lovers, he liked being close, liked staying up late and carrying her to her bed when she fell asleep on his lap in front of the TV. Jesus, he liked everything about her, always had and always would, and even though they had a bond, a connection they didn't seem to share with anyone but each other, it seemed to have grown, intensified under their ruse.

Since he couldn't seem to concentrate on anything other than her, he closed the book in front of him and pinched the bridge of his nose. Soon enough she'd be turning to Caleb for comfort, not him. His stomach soured but he fought down the jealousy rising in him. Caleb was a good guy, and good for her. That's what was important.

His phone pinged and he pulled it from his pocket to read a message from Caleb. *I'm here.* He grabbed his backpack, shoved his books inside and stood just as Caleb came in through the front door. He headed straight for Sky, and Matt sat back down on his stool as he approached her, arms open.

"Hey, Skywalker," Caleb said, pulling her in for a hug. He lifted her off her feet and squeezed. She made a small sound as he lowered her. Hands still braced on the small of her back, he inched back and looked her over. "You okay?"

She nodded and put her arms around him as he continued to hold her. "I'm fine. Thanks to Matt."

Caleb grinned. "You mean *Simon's* fine, thanks to Matt."

He gestured toward the bat under the bar. "I've seen you swing." He let her go, made a fist and nudged her chin. "You would have cleaned his clock."

Sky's hands fell to her sides, and Matt didn't miss the look that came over her when Caleb gave her a bump like she was one of the guys. She opened her mouth and closed it, like she wasn't sure what to say next.

"All set?" Matt asked, coming to her rescue.

"Yeah."

Caleb grabbed his keys from his pocket and started swinging them around his finger. Matt walked around the counter and put his mouth close to Sky's ear. "You going to be okay if I take off for a while?"

"Sure," With a nod she gestured toward his friends at the pool table. "The place is packed with guys who'd kick Simon's ass for me."

"Okay, if you need me just text and I'll be here."

She put her hand on his chest, and said, "Go. Drink beer with Thor, and stop worrying about me."

"Thor?" he asked.

"I mean Theo." She laughed and pointed to Kat and a few of her friends sitting at one of the tables. "Kat calls him Thor."

Matt grinned and closed his hand over hers as it lingered on his chest. "I think she just might have met her match with that guy."

She wet her lips and his gaze fell to her mouth. His pulse kicked up a notch, and if he wasn't mistaken her breath seemed to come a little quicker.

"I'll be back for lock-up," he said.

Her tongue darted out to swipe over her bottom lip again, and temptation swamped him. Jesus Christ, the last thing he should be doing was loving the idea of kissing her again.

He commanded himself to get it together and walk away

without taking what he wanted, but when she exhaled a shuddery breath, and he caught her sweetness, all rational thought fled. He dipped his head and pressed his lips to hers. At first her mouth was stiff, but when he angled his head and made a slow pass with his tongue, her entire body softened. A groan caught in his throat as she kissed him back. Jesus, the things this woman did to him without even trying. Her hand pressed against his chest and curled in his shirt. Longing ripped through him as his mind sifted through all the ways he wanted to take her. But when someone from behind cleared their throat, he pulled back.

A strange wheezing sound rose from her throat. "What... what was that for?"

He pulled in a fortifying breath. "Audience," he lied.

"Oh." She turned and looked at Caleb, who was standing there blatantly staring at them.

"I'll catch up with you later," he said and brushed his thumb over her bottom lip. Matt stepped out from behind the bar to discover more than just Caleb gawking. Kat and her crew from the hospital were all seated around the table watching, but the look in Kat's eyes unnerved him. What was that Jack has said? That he wasn't the only one who knew how much he liked Sky. Did Kat know how he really felt?

He pushed through the doors and walked with Caleb to his truck. Caleb climbed in and looked at him. He shook his head and started the engine. "I'm not sure if I'll ever get used to the idea of you two together."

"We thought we'd give it a try. See where it led."

"And how's that working out for you?"

He looked at his friend, who'd given him the perfect opening to set the stage for their breakup. "She's beautiful, isn't she?"

"Yeah, I guess she is." He put the truck into gear and exited the parking lot. "I never really noticed before."

"Sweet too. Any guy would be lucky to have her." He laughed. "She sends food to Gran all the time." He shook his head. "Gran thinks it's time me and Sky settle down."

"Ah, so that's what's gotten under your skin lately. Gran's been pushing you to get married. I knew something was up with you."

"Sky and I go way back, so I thought..."

"That she could be the one?"

"Did you ever think about going out with her?"

"Not until you did, but I guess I missed my chance, she's your girl now."

Staring straight again, Matt tried to keep his expression blank, tried not to give away the apprehension churning inside him as Caleb drove to Theo's place. They were good together, he reminded himself.

You want her to be happy. Caleb makes her happy. But you're going to lose her.

He was all kinds of fucked up when Caleb pulled in behind Cole Sullivan and Brad Crosby. All talk of Sky ended as they met Cole and Brad in the driveway and the four made their way inside to play cards and kick back with Theo.

They let themselves in, and when they reached the kitchen, Theo jumped up from his chair. He balanced on his cane, grabbed four beers from the fridge and handed them out.

"How's it going?" Matt asked, glancing downward to take in the battle scars on his friend's leg. "I hear Kat is doing great things with you."

Theo grinned and ran his hand over his face like he was in pure agony. "Great things? She's a damn masochist. Relentless too."

"You're smitten," Matt said.

"Channeling Gran again," Caleb shot out from the other end of the table.

The guys all laughed and Matt grabbed a chair and twisted the cap off his beer. He put it between his fingers and snapped them. The cap zipped through the air and caught Caleb on the forehead.

Caleb winced. "Jesus, man. It's all fun and games until you put an eye out."

"Now who's channeling Gran."

Cole grabbed the cards and stared dealing. "You two are like an old married couple."

"Look who's talking," Caleb returned. "If anyone should know about being an old married couple it's you and Gemma."

"And never been happier," he said with a grin. "You should be so lucky."

"I hear Matt's the lucky one," Brad said, tipping his bottle to his mouth. "About time you got together with Sky."

"Yeah," Matt mumbled and stared at his cards. "That's what I keep hearing."

Caleb shook his head and leaned back in his seat, balancing on the two back legs of the chair. With his hand in front of his neck and fingers outstretched, he swung it back and forth. "Cut it out. All this talk about married couples is giving me a rash."

"What do you have against marriage?" Cole asked.

Caleb gathered his cards and flicked the corner of one against the table. "Nothing." He smirked at Matt and a thud sounded when he went back down on all four legs. "But now that the sweetest girl I know is taken, looks like I'll forever be single." As everyone stared at him—like he had no idea what he was missing out on—he turned to Theo, the only other single guy in the room. Or so everyone thought. "You want to help me out here?" he asked him.

"Ah...no."

Soon enough the ribbing started in on Theo, the guys

wanting to hear all about his *physical* therapy with Kat. Matt shifted his cards around in his hands, happy that the attention was off him and Sky. There were a couple of well-trained soldiers in the room who could read him like an open book and he didn't want them to know what was really going on inside his head.

The front door opened and closed, and he turned to see who was joining them. Speaking of well-trained soldiers who could read others. "Hey," Jack called out as his Shepherd, Colby, came racing into the kitchen. He walked from soldier to soldier, getting his fair share of attention, then plunked himself at Jack's feet when he grabbed a chair.

"Sorry I'm late, I got caught up at the compound."

"As soon as I get fixed up, I'll be there to help out," Theo said, standing to grab Jack a beer from the fridge.

"You worry about getting that leg better," Jack said, twisting the top off and taking a long pull. "We have enough help for now."

Even though Matt was busy, he always made time to go to the compound to help his comrades train dogs to put them in the hands of soldiers who were working to defuse munitions that had been left over from former training camps during the wars. The whole idea had been Cole's and the dogs came from his wife's no-kill shelter. Matt had become particularly fond of Murphy, even though he was an older dog that liked to chase birds and rarely took orders. He laughed as he thought about him. The damn mutt had a mind of his own, and Matt was pretty certain he'd be better off as someone's pet. If he had the room, he'd take him in himself. Then again, even if he had the room his apartment was pet-free.

"I've been making great progress with Ruby," Caleb said.

Cole laughed. "Yeah, I heard she's kind of sweet on you."

"Who isn't?" Jack said, laughing, as his shrewd gaze drifted to Matt.

"Yeah, I'll be by too," Matt said, throwing his cards down for a reshuffle now that Jack was there. "So are we going to play cards or what?"

All attention turned to the game and Matt nursed his beer as the night progressed. He kept a close eye on his watch, wanting to be back at the bar before Sky closed up. When his phone rang, his heart jumped into his throat. *Sky.*

He pulled it from his pocket but didn't recognize the number. Jumping from his seat he stepped into the other room so he could hear over the guys, and what he heard just about stopped his heart. He listened to the details, then shoved his phone back into his pocket.

"Caleb, I need your keys."

Caleb fished his keys from his pocket and handed them to him. "What's going on?"

"That was the hospital. Gran fell again. She fractured her hip."

Caleb pushed back from the table. "I'll drive."

"No. I need you to make sure Sky gets home okay. I'll text you from the hospital when I know more."

"Yeah, of course," Caleb said.

Matt took off outside and jumped into Caleb's truck. He sped through the streets and pulled into a parking space in front of the Emergency entrance at the hospital. He jammed the vehicle into Park and rushed inside. He raced to the receptionist, who told him where his Gran was. He walked the long length of the hall, the scent of antiseptic tickling his nostrils. A nurse hurried by with a tray of blood-filled tubes, and when he found Gran's room, he slowed his steps, not wanting to appear anxious and upset her any more than she was. He stepped in, and glanced at the nurse as she finished prepping Gran for surgery.

"You're just in time," the nurse said quietly.

He looked at Gran and his throat tightened. He wished

she'd go into the nursing home so she'd have around-the-clock care like he wanted, but she refused, insisting she could do everything on her own. While it was true, and she could still get around on her own, he didn't like the idea of her rattling around in that old house by herself. He thought about moving in with her, but the place held nothing but bad memories.

"Matt," Gran said, reaching out to him.

Taking her hand in his, he leaned over her. From the glassy look in her eyes, he could tell the pain meds had already been administered. "How are you feeling, Gran?"

"Like an old fool," she said, and Matt smiled, happy to see she was still her feisty self. "I was reaching for the box of tissue and Dexter got under foot. It's not his fault though. He just never likes to leave my side when I'm sick."

A noise at the door had him glancing up to see two orderlies rolling in a gurney. Matt gave Gran's hand a squeeze. "They're taking you for surgery now, Gran. I'll be here when you get out."

"I need you to check on the cats," she said.

"I will, don't worry."

He stood back as they transferred her to the other bed. Once she was situated, he gave her a kiss on the forehead. They rolled her into the hall and as she disappeared around the corner, he turned to the nurse. "How long will it take?"

"The doctor will be by to explain everything." She waved her hand toward the door. "Come with me. I'll get you settled in the lounge."

He followed her down the hall to a lounge room with nice seating and a TV on the wall. Newspapers and magazines lined the coffee table, but there was no way he could focus enough to read. A man and woman, who looked to be in their late fifties, held hands as they sat staring at the TV and he could only assume they too were waiting for news on a loved one.

He paced until the doctor came by, and after he filled Matt in on the procedure, Matt dropped down into one of the chairs. Bracing his elbows on his knees he leaned forward and rested his forehead on his palms. He stayed in that position for a long time, until he heard his name.

He glanced up to see Sky rushing toward him.

"Sky, what are you doing here?" He looked past her shoulder to see Caleb walking behind her with a nurse at his side.

"Cole dropped us off. I came as soon as I heard." She put her arms around him and gave him a hug.

He hugged her back, burying his face in her hair. "You didn't have to come."

"Of course I did. How is Gran?"

"She's in surgery."

"Hey," Caleb said, putting his hand on Matt's shoulder. "You okay?" Matt nodded. "Good, I'll go see if I can find anything out."

Caleb walked to the nursing station, and Matt turned his attention back to Sky. "She tripped on Dexter."

Sky nodded. "She's going to be, okay. I just know it."

"I hate her being in that house alone."

"She wants to keep her independence."

"I should move in with her."

Sky nodded again and reached for his hand. No words needed to be said, because she knew what the house meant to him, and what it didn't. She tugged on him. "Let's sit." He closed both his hands over hers and just held her. Caleb came back with three paper cups filled with coffee and a handful of cream and sugar.

He handed them to Sky. "I wasn't sure how you wanted it." She gathered up the condiments and Caleb turned to

Matt. "No news yet," he said. "But that's a good thing, Matt. I'm sure it's a textbook surgery and Gran will be herself in no time at all."

Matt nodded his appreciation and took a sip of his coffee while Sky doctored hers. They made small talk and stared at the TV for the next few hours, and when the doctor finally came to see him they all jumped to their feet.

"Matt," the doctor said. "Your grandmother is doing just fine. Surgery went well and she is resting."

Matt nearly sobbed with relief. "Can I see her?"

"No, she'll be in recovery for some time. The best thing you can do is go home and get some rest. Come back tomorrow. You'll be able to see her then."

"I'll just wait."

"Come on, Matt," Caleb said, being his voice of reason. "The best thing you can do for Gran is get some sleep. She's not going to want you up all night worrying."

"He's right," Sky said. "Let's go home."

He nodded and Sky put her arm around his waist as they made their way back to Caleb's truck. He handed the keys over to Caleb and Sky shuffled into the middle between them. The streets were quiet this time of night, and he stifled a yawn as exhaustion pulled at him. When the vehicle stopped he looked down and that's when he realized he'd been holding Sky's hand this entire drive. She kept shooting glances his way and he finally looked at her.

"I'm okay," he said.

She nodded as Caleb pulled up in front of the building instead of grabbing one of the guest parking spots.

"Aren't you coming in?" Matt asked.

Caleb tapped the wheel. "I think I'm going to take off."

Matt pulled open his door and slid from the truck. "It's late. You're tired. Just crash at my place."

"I'm good," Caleb said. Matt put his arm on the top of the

open door, waiting for Sky. Caleb leaned into Sky and whispered something into her ear before dropping a kiss onto her cheek.

She nodded in response to whatever he'd said. "You sure you shouldn't just sleep here?"

"I have rounds early tomorrow, and I'll sleep better in my own bed. Keep me posted if you hear anything from Gran though."

"Okay. I'll text you."

Sky followed Matt inside and up the stairs to their floor. He unlocked his door and she followed him inside.

He turned to her. "Thanks for coming tonight."

"Of course. I wanted to be there for you and Gran."

She really was the sweetest girl he knew. Her hand went to his hair and she pushed it from his face. He leaned into her, his emotions a hot fucking mess. The thought of losing Gran scared the living crap out of him, and as he looked at Sky now, he knew when she hooked up with Caleb, he was definitely going to lose her.

"Sky," he murmured as she regarded him with wide eyes. With his nerves strung so tight, he knew she needed to go, otherwise he could very well snap, and end up doing something there would be no coming back from. "It's late. You should go."

"I'm not going anywhere." She put her arms around him again and hugged tight. With her face against his chest, she murmured, "I'm staying with you tonight."

A groan caught in his throat, and due to his current mood, he knew he couldn't have her close tonight, not without either going batshit crazy or helping himself to a small taste. With every intention of turning her around and pointing her toward the door, he gripped her shoulders and inched backward, putting a small measure of distance between them. She tilted her head to see him. Her mouth parted and confusion danced in her dark eyes as he shoved her away. Fuck, how could he possibly think straight when she looked at him like that? His fingers tightened on her shoulders and, as need ripped through him, he suddenly found himself drawing her back to him. Sure, there was a huge list of concrete reasons why being with her was wrong. Too bad he couldn't remember a goddamn single one of them.

———

Ohmygod.

Matt was kissing her. His mouth was on hers, his lips moving urgently as his hands left her shoulders to slide down her back. He pulled her in tight, and she could feel his arousal against her stomach as his body pressed hard. A tremble moved through her despite the warmth in the room. Clearly she'd been without a man too long, otherwise she wouldn't be acting this way...with Matt.

A moan filled the silence between them. She listened to it linger in the air, then drift away. Another moan sounded and that's when she realized the sound was coming from *her* throat. In the dark of the night, without an audience, Matt was kissing her and *she* was the one moaning.

Her brain stalled, then raced to catch up. She should stop this. She really should. Clearly he was reaching out to her because his emotions were a hot mess, and this had to be some sort of reaction to the stress. But when his tongue slid inside to play with hers, so skilled and needy, her thoughts fragmented, focusing only on how sweet he tasted, how hard and hot his body felt pressed against her.

He angled his head and deepened the kiss, and as though moving of their own accord, her hands went around his sides. As she acknowledged the flare of desire between her legs, she grabbed his shirt and tugged, pulling it away from his body.

This time the moan came from him. She slipped her hands under the soft cotton, loving the feel of his hard-packed muscles beneath her fingers. Her palms raced over his back, and a shudder moved through him.

Some small, working brain cell told her this wasn't rational, or smart, but before she could listen to it, Matt picked her up and carried her to his room. He tossed her onto the unmade bed, caveman style, and she gasped when she caught the intensity in his gaze. They shared a long, heated look, one that caused her body to quiver from head to toe. Lust twisted inside her and she bit back a breathy moan.

Oh God, was this happening? Was this really happening? She opened her mouth to ask, but when a growl rumbled in Matt's throat and he put a burning hand on her neck, running it all the way down to the apex between her legs, she went silent, knowing there was no way she could form a coherent sentence. His hand lingered between her thighs for a moment, then traveled back up her body. He caressed her skin, softly, barely touching, but at the same time making her so aware of him, and his hard body.

Good God, someone ought to stick a space-for-rent sign right on her forehead, because the feel of his fingers on her flesh had just killed her last working brain cell. With need ruling her actions, she met his glance and sucked in a sharp breath.

Looking dark, dangerous and wild—like he'd checked his gentlemanly ways at the door—he gripped the back of his shirt and peeled it over his head. Her sex fluttered in response, registering every little detail while she looked her fill, staring blatantly. Her perusal paused briefly on the hard outline straining against his jeans. A near-violent tremor moved though her as she took in his nakedness. He was so beautiful. How come she'd never noticed before?

Her gaze went back to his and his eyes burned into hers,

igniting every nerve ending inside her. His jaw clenched and his nostrils flared as he closed the gap between them. He knelt on the bed and sexual tension flared between them. He fell over her and she bent her legs at the knees and widened them to accommodate his girth. He settled himself on top of her, and his weight pinned her to the bed. His lips crashed down on hers again, and he kissed her hard, possessively, his tongue demanding more—everything—as it slipped inside her mouth.

He took possession of her body, and as she looked at him it occurred to her this was no longer the Matt she knew. But that didn't mean she disliked this side. She didn't. Not by a long shot. Desperate to explore, she put her arms around his back and his muscles bunched beneath her touch. Exhaling a shallow breath, she continued her exploration as his mouth left hers. He buried his face in the hollow of her throat and shifted his weight, gripping both her arms to pin her hands over her head. He wrapped her fingers around the slats in his headboard.

"Keep them there," he growled into her throat, his deep voice making her toes curl.

Oh God...

As heat flooded her sex and her body beckoned his touch, his hands tugged at her shirt, pushing it up over her bra. Without bothering to release the latch, he hauled the cups down to expose her breasts. A rich, decadent rumble filled the room and his warm breath fell over her bare skin as he sucked in air and let it out slowly.

"So beautiful." He brushed the underside with rough fingers, then leaned in to draw one hard nipple into his mouth. Sky lifted her head to watch, but when he sucked hard, and then none-too-gently bit down, her head fell back onto the pillow. He brushed his tongue over her nipple, as if to soothe the sting left behind.

"So good," she murmured.

His mouth went to her other nipple, giving it the same mind-numbing treatment until she lifted her hips, pressing her sex against him. She moved, grinding herself on the hard planes of his stomach, her body desperate for so much more.

His hands bit into her hips. "Stay still."

She stopped moving—breathing—as he went all alpha on her, taking charge of their play...her body. His hand slipped between them and he fingered the button on her jeans before pushing it through the hole. The hiss of her zipper cut the silence and with her thoughts spiraling out of control, she rocked against him, conveying without words what she wanted.

Once again, his hand splayed over her stomach to still her, and when his eyes met hers they darkened to a color she'd never before seen. "Don't worry," he said, the depth of certainty in his voice arousing her even more. "I've got this."

The promise she spotted backlighting his eyes had antici-pation careening through her blood, and her body moistened all over. Her lids fell shut, a strangled moan catching in her throat as he slid down her body. He dropped a sprinkling of hot kisses onto her stomach, and she listened to his intake of breath, like he was breathing in the scent of her skin.

His mouth met her jeans, and she squirmed as he went back on his heels. He gripped the sides and tugged them down her legs, leaving her in her white lace panties. He tossed her clothes away, his tongue trailing back up her thighs as he squeezed her legs together—hard. Oh God, the force pinched her swollen clit and when she moaned, she was sure she heard a rumble of laughter in his throat—a clear sign that he knew exactly what he was doing. Blindsided by lust as he fed the intensity of her arousal, her lids flicked back open to find him looking at her.

With their eyes locked, he fingered the material on her

panties, then ripped them clear from her hips. Her mouth formed a little O but no words came as he tossed the slip of material away. He angled his head, like he dared her to say something, but when she kept quiet his gaze dropped.

"Open for me," he commanded, his voice dropping an octave.

She did as requested and he took a long time to stare at her sex, longer than was comfortable. She was about to cover herself when he reached out and parted her with his fingers, stroking all the way from bottom to top, nudging her clit along the way.

"How can you be so wet?" he murmured between clenched teeth, and briefly pinched his eyes shut as if he were in sweet agony. "I haven't even touched you yet."

Shivers skittered along her spine as he stroked her and when she writhed on the mattress, he gripped both legs and spread them even more. Leaning forward he pressed his mouth to her pubis. His lips were hot on her skin as he repositioned himself. He made a slow, skilled pass with his tongue, and that first sweet touch to her pussy had her hips coming off the bed.

"Yes," she cried out, and held the slats tighter. He circled her clit with his tongue as he manipulated it with his thumb. It was the most delicious thing she'd ever felt. She tossed her head from side to side, her body trembling, her muscles tightening. Matt never swore around her but she was pretty sure he was mumbling curses from between her legs. His teeth clamped around her clit and she surrendered to the pleasure, wiggling beneath the play of his tongue as the tang of her arousal reached her nostrils.

He sucked harder, and her thoughts became a swirling vortex of need. "Please..." she begged even though she had no idea what she was begging for.

Moving with urgency, he pulled her hands from the slats

and with little finesse he grabbed her by the hips and flipped her over. She gasped at his roughness, the forceful way he was taking charge. She might be a vanilla girl, one who'd never been taken like this before, but she couldn't deny that she liked it. A lot.

The hairs on his arm tickled her sensitized skin as he slipped a hand around her waist to adjust her body. He lifted her slightly and stuffed a pillow under her stomach, tipping her ass up in the air toward him. *Oh my!* He lay over her and need flared between her legs as he pressed his hardness between her cheeks. His other hand went to the middle of her back. He dragged his fingers down her spine, going all the way to her bare backside. He cupped one cheek and then, taking her by surprise, she felt his palm come down over her.

"Oh," she cried out. Good God, Matt had just spanked her, and she liked it. A beat passed and then he did it again, sending ripples of sensual pleasure surging through her. His breathing changed, became harsher, and fueled by need she said, "Please..."

"Please what?"

She opened her mouth and closed it again, unable to keep a focused thought as he squeezed her cheek like it was pliable dough. She had no idea Matt was a man who took no prisoners in the bedroom and played by his own rules. Okay, maybe that wasn't entirely true. Thanks to Kat she *did* have an inkling of an idea and, if she was being totally honest with herself, the thoughts of Matt and kink in the same sentence had intrigued her. Otherwise she might have put a stop to this while she still could. All along she believed stable and kind trumped wild, untamed sex, but holy hell this alpha take-charge attitude was messing with her body and her brain.

He put his hand between her legs and plunged a thick finger inside her. "Is this what you want?"

Her body convulsed and he gripped her around the waist to absorb her tremor. Since a reply was beyond her, she pinched her lips tight and reached out to grab the slats. That action seemed to do something to him because he suddenly went quiet, his finger stilling inside her.

Her body hummed with excitement and she waited for him to work his finger in and out of her, to ease the escalating tension, but no movement came. She nearly sobbed with want. Was he trying to kill her? Wanting—needing—more, she rocked against his finger, but stopped when she felt a palm come down over her ass. *Yes!* Her sex clenched hard, and Matt groaned.

"Don't move," he growled, giving her ass another hard whack before he cupped her cheek and squeezed. He pushed another finger inside and she buried her face in the sheets as he filled her.

Oh God, it felt so good.

She listened to his harsh breathing as he moved his fingers, drawing them all the way out only to plunge back in again. Tension built inside her, her body screaming for release. It was blissful torture. She wanted to push against him but didn't dare move for fear of him stopping, but she soon found excitement in following his rules.

His fingers moved faster, stroking the hot bundle of nerves inside. She swallowed as tension grew, coming to a peak. Her sex squeezed around his fingers, and she dragged in a breath as her body let go. Ripples of pleasure traveled onward and outward, and he remained between her legs, licking and stroking and drawing out her pleasure until the spasms stopped. He petted her sex softly, and she took that time to figure out how to breathe again. As she took deep, gulping breaths, he climbed from the bed.

He tore his pants off, his eyes flaring hot as he reached into the nightstand. Lacking any sort of modesty he stood beside the bed completely naked, and in her haze of arousal she took her time to look him over. Her gaze left a sculpted stomach and moved downward to take in his cock. She swallowed against the sudden dryness in her throat when she saw his length and girth. He was so big, hard and ready, and as she stared, she watched it grow harder. A cry lodged in her throat and her fingers tingled, wanting to reach out and touch him. She closed her eyes against the flood of heat but opened them again when he slammed the nightstand drawer shut.

He gripped his cock, fisting it at the base, and as his muscles rippled, she was sure she'd never seen anything sexier. The foil package went to his mouth and he ripped into it with his teeth. God, he looked so wild, so feral, it excited her as much as it frightened her. His gaze caressed her body, and fixated on her bare backside. She wiggled slightly, urging him on, and the warning look he gave her had her pulse jumping.

Primed and ready, he slid back over her and she could feel his crown probing her opening. He gripped her hips and lifted her ass a bit higher, and her thoughts fell apart as he pitched forward, driving all the way inside her. His breath came in a ragged burst as he filled her with every glorious inch. And, oh, what a lot of inches he had.

She gave a breathy moan. "Yes," she whispered with effort as their bodies fused together.

Like a man on a mission he began powering his hips forward, exploring her deeper. As her hair tumbled across the mattress, he moved urgently over her, plunging harder, faster and she buried her face in the sheets, breathing in the warm scent of him. Growls rumbled from behind as he speared her with his cock, pounding her into the mattress with each forceful thrust. Her nipples scraped against the bedding as he reached a fevered pitch, pounding hard, bruising her body in ways that excited her beyond anything she'd ever known.

She could feel the tension rising in him—in her—as he

rode furiously. She felt him shift his position, angling for deeper thrusts. The depth of penetration as he stroked with hunger, with expertise, stole the breath from her lungs.

He brushed his lips over her back, and as her body absorbed the heat from his mouth, a shudder overcame her. He fell over her, gripping her shoulders with one hand as the other slipped between her pelvis and the pillow. He touched her clit and she pushed against his hand, desperate...so damn desperate. He stroked her hard as he continued to drive into her and the dual pressure pushed her to the edge a second time. Hot sparks shot through her body and he must have felt them.

"Come for me," he demanded, his voice playing down her spine.

His tongue skated across her neck, and the delicious scent of his skin swirled around her. Heat flowed through her blood, thick and heavy, and when he growled into her ear, another orgasm hit hard.

Matt growled as her cream dripped down her thighs, her liquid heat lubricating them even more. His hips jerked forward once, twice, and a second later he grabbed a fistful of her hair and stilled his movements. Sky stopped breathing as he pulsed inside her, his pleasure resonating through her entire body. Her muscles spasmed, sucking him in deeper, and he gave a tug on her hair. She closed her eyes to enjoy the sensations rocketing through her.

He stayed on top of her for a long time, his heart beating hard against her back. His breath fell over her, warm and sweet as he took her hands from the slats. He placed them beside her head and put his palms over them, a tenderness in his touch as he brushed his thumb over hers.

"Sky?"

"Yeah," she said, soaking in his warmth.

"Are you okay?" A wave of heat moved through her at the

softness in his voice, but beneath that softness she heard something else, something that sounded like regret.

"I am. You?"

"I...yeah."

He rolled off her, discarded the condom and snatched the pillow out from her hips. He put it back in place, grabbed her and pulled her next to him. She nestled against him and thought about how nice it was to be held by him as he pulled the bedding over their bodies. His fingers played down her arm as hers went to her bruised lips, running over the events of the night. No man had ever touched her or kissed her with such ferocity, such passion. As she thought about that, she shifted, and felt his strong heart pound hard against her cheek. That's when she realized he was quiet. Too quiet.

She angled her chin and stole a quick glance at him to find him staring at the ceiling. Unease moved through her when she caught the worry on his face, and he stopped running his finger along her arm, leaving cold where there was once warmth. Her throat dried, and her mind raced, trying to figure out where they went from here. She wanted to say something, anything, to address his concern, but what could she possibly say? What they did might have felt right, but as the lust cleared from her head, she knew it wasn't. Matt was her best friend. A guy who was pretending to be her boyfriend so she could open another man's eyes.

She thought their ruse would only involve kissing and touching. Thought it wouldn't affect her. But this... Holy hell...they'd crossed a line tonight and the truth was not only did it affect her, it had her wanting more.

8

Early-morning sun slanted in through the curtains. He'd lain in bed staring at the ceiling for the better part of the night, his body tired but his mind too keyed up to sleep. Neither of them spoke after he pulled out of her a few hours ago. Silence lingered between them, both lost in their own thoughts. He briefly pinched his eyes shut, not wanting to think about what was going through her mind after the lust had cleared.

He shook his head, angry with himself. He'd crossed a line with her, one that he never should have crossed. What the hell had he been thinking? He should have walked away, should have pointed her to the door and forced her to leave, but goddammit when she put her arms around him, her body teasing and tormenting his to the point of no return, he lost all ability to think rationally. And then what did he do? He'd tossed her onto the bed and went at her like a fucking rutting animal. He'd been so rough, so needy, even pinning her hands above her head and demanding she not move them.

And why did you do that, dude?

But he already knew the answer. He'd wanted her so bad

for so long now, that the feel of her fingers on his skin, touching softly, exploring thoroughly, nearly did him in. If he'd allowed her to continue caressing his body he knew he would have blown like a grenade, ending things before they even began—which is exactly what he should have done.

He glanced down to see her hair sprawled across his chest. He fought the desire to touch her again, to push her hair from her face and find her lips. He could tell by her breathing that she was awake. He needed to talk to her, to make things right between them, because he was pretty certain in the light of day, they both knew last night never should have happened.

"Sky?"

"Yeah." Her hand went to his chest and she widened her fingers.

He closed his hand over hers and put it back by her side. He couldn't have her touching him again, otherwise he'd lose it and fuck knows what he'd do then. Things were already fucked up enough, and he could at least blame last night on the strain he'd been under.

Worry crept into his voice when he said, "I'm sorry."

Her hair fell over his shoulder as she tipped her head to see him. She opened her mouth, closed it, then opened it again. "I...I..." she began, but he pressed his fingers to her lips.

"It's okay. You don't have to say anything. We both know this never should have happened and, believe me, the fault is all mine, not yours." He shook his head and thought back to last night, to when his emotions were running high. "I just...I wasn't in my right mind."

"I know," she whispered and looked down, her lids masking her emotions.

Even though he could tell she didn't want to pursue this conversation and was undoubtedly feeling the regret every bit as much as he was, he cupped her chin and lifted it until their eyes met. Sure the sex had been great and he felt her come—twice—but they needed to clear the air and make things right between them. Christ, if he lost her because of his stupidity... His glance moved over her face and his gut clenched with the apprehension he met there. If he had the ability to kick his own ass for being such a greedy prick, he'd already have had size-twelve boot print bruising it.

"I'm sorry." His voice hitched and he tried again. "I'm so sorry, Sky."

"It's okay."

He looked at her shirt and thought about the way he'd tugged her bra down. Disgusted with himself for not having the decency to undress her properly, he shook his head. "It's not okay and I can't believe the way I...the way I took you." Not only did he leave her half-dressed, he'd flipped her over and had even slapped her ass a few times. Holy fuck. He might be a little rough between the sheets, less than refined inside the bedroom, but she didn't deserve to be held down hard and taken from any guy, let alone him.

She averted her gaze and toyed with the edge of the bed sheet, like she needed to busy her hands.

Desperate to move past this, he gripped a fistful of his hair and said, "I think we should just forget this ever happened, okay?" Yeah, like he could ever forget the taste of her body, the way she came in his mouth, the feel of her tight pussy squeezing his cock as he let go high inside her. He sucked in a quick breath as the sheets began to tent.

"Okay?" she croaked out, covering herself with the blanket. "It was a mistake. I get it. We were both upset. Neither one of us were thinking right."

Even though he'd already seen her naked, he said, "I'll leave so you can get dressed."

"But you already..." Her words fell off when he slipped

from the bed to pull on his jeans. He turned back around to see her staring at his chest.

He sat on the edge of the mattress, keeping a measure of distance from her as unease raced through his veins. How could he have been such a dumbass? "Please tell me this isn't going to come between us." He pinched the bridge of his nose. "I don't...I can't..." Before he could get the words out his cell phone pinged. He grabbed it from his back pocket, and swallowed hard. "It's Caleb, asking about Gran." He sent back a message, then looked at Sky. "I'm going to check on her cats and then go see her, okay?" He wondered how she'd take that. Any other day she'd go with him, but after last night would she run the other way.

"I'll need a quick shower and a change of clothes," she said, the normalcy in her voice, her actions, filling him with relief. "I also wanted to bring some lunch to the guys at the base afterward. Can you give me fifteen minutes to get ready?"

His heart squeezed, because this was the sweet Sky he knew and loved, not the one who looked at him with grief after a night that shouldn't have happened.

"Yeah, I need to shower too. And I told Jack I'd help out today so I'll help you with the food." He pushed his hair from his face and when his phone pinged again, he glanced at the screen. "Caleb is heading to the base later, after rounds."

"Oh," she said, glancing down again.

"Do you think...?"

She looked back up at him. "Do I think what?"

"Do you think we should plan that breakup today?"

She went quiet for a long time, and she looked past his shoulder toward the window, like she was deep in thought.

"Sky?" he said, dragging her focus back to him.

She nodded and met his glance. "Okay. I think that would be for the best."

"How do you want to do it?"

"I don't want to make a big public scene." She crinkled her nose. "Maybe you could just tell the guys it didn't work out."

He nodded, and knew there were far too many hard-core soldiers who were trained to read others. They'd undoubtedly see right through his act. But what choice did he have? She wasn't his.

"Okay," he agreed. "I'll make sure Caleb knows we're done and hint that the two of you would make a better pair." He pushed off the bed and grabbed Sky's jeans from the floor. When he saw her torn panties, he cringed. He picked them up and placed them on top of her jeans. A noise caught in Sky's throat and when he glanced at her, he noticed the stain of embarrassment on her face.

Shit. "I...uh...sorry. I'll replace them."

She arched one brow. "Are you going to go underwear shopping at Victoria's Secret, Matt?" she asked and he could tell she was trying to lighten the mood. He'd fucked up with her, yet she was coming to his rescue. No wonder he loved her so much.

"Yeah, I am. I ripped your panties, and I will replace them. It's the least I can do."

She touched her frayed underwear, "Do you...? Are you always...?"

"Am I always what?"

"You know. That...intense."

Intense? He guessed that was one way to look at it. "I didn't mean to lose it like that, Sky."

"I just never saw that side of you before."

"That's because we've never slept together."

"Oh," she said, the color on her cheeks deepening.

"Look, I'm sorry. I shouldn't have been so rough with you."

"You don't have anything to be sorry for."

He wasn't sure what she meant by that, and while they were always open with each other, talking about everything, he wanted to end this conversation before he made things worse. "I'm going to jump in the shower," he said and made a beeline for the door.

He listened to the bedsheets rustle as he left the room. He closed the bathroom door behind him and leaned against it, waiting for her to leave the apartment. The front door clicked shut and he reached into the shower, turning the water to hot. He undressed and climbed in. Desperate to wash her from his skin, his brain, he grabbed the soap and scrubbed until his flesh was practically raw.

He climbed out, dried off and tugged on a clean pair of jeans and T-shirt. Stepping into his kitchen, he grabbed a slice of bread and spread on a thick layer of peanut butter. He munched on it as he crossed the hall. Using his key, he let himself in, and plunked himself down on her sofa until she was ready. He looked at the torn underwear she left on her coffee table and nearly choked on his bread.

Darting to her kitchen, he grabbed the orange juice and took a swig from the container.

"Hey, you're spreading germs."

"Oops, sorry." He held it out to her. "Want some?"

She took the carton from him and he caught a whiff of her skin. He clenched down to stifle a groan.

"Since we probably share all the same ones anyway, why not." She put it to her lips and drank and that's when he realized she was still in a towel, her wet hair falling over her shoulders. She handed it back and made a face that looked like she'd just sucked on a lemon. "It tastes like peanut butter."

"Breakfast of champions."

"That's debatable." She shook her head, and he was so

happy to see things between them were normal. At least as normal as they could be under the circumstances. Hell, maybe they could have sex again and again, and carry on like nothing had ever happened afterward.

"You want something to eat?"

"Yeah, put a slice in for me, and just a skim of butter." She turned and disappeared down the hall. When she stepped into her bedroom, he tore his gaze away and adjusted his pants. He stuck her bread in the toaster and when it popped he buttered it like she wanted. Sky came back out wearing a mid-thigh white skirt that showcased her gorgeous legs, and a T-shirt that hugged her breasts. Honest to God, even though she was all grown up some days she looked like she was still teenager. She wasn't, but she sure as hell made him feel like a fourteen-year-old boy at times—hard and horny.

He handed her the toast and she grabbed her keys from the bowl she kept on her kitchen table. "I'll drive," she said. "I won't be able to bring the guys food on your bike. Plus, I'm in a skirt."

He nodded and left the room, happy to let her drive. The thoughts of her on the back of his bike, those long sexy legs of hers wrapped around his body, was more than he could take right now.

They hopped into her car and made the short trip to Gran's house. He fished the key from his pocket and pushed the door open for Sky to enter first. Meowing could be heard as he followed her in.

"Hey, Dexter," Sky said, bending down to pick him up. "Poor baby. You must be worried about Gran too."

She ran her hands over his fur, and the cat meowed louder. Matt stepped past them and padded down the hall to the kitchen. Two cats jumped from the sofa and followed him.

Sky leaned against the counter beside him. "How many cats does she have now?"

"Three." He grabbed the can opener and three tins of food from the cupboard. "Which is three too many if you ask me."

"Dog guy. Right. I got it." Dexter leapt from her hands, and went to his bowl. As Matt dished out the food, Sky folded her arms and sauntered into the living room. "You need to change the cat litter," she called out, her voice echoing in the quiet house.

"Why do you think I brought you along?" he countered.

"Forget it, Matt."

"Come on, Sky. You know I hate changing the litter."

She poked her head around the corner to see him. "What will you give me?" she asked, and he couldn't help but laugh at their childhood game.

"I'll make your bed for one whole week."

She grinned. "Not good enough."

"Okay, I'll do your dishes too."

"I have a dishwasher."

"I'm not vacuuming." He dropped the empty tins into the garbage can and ran his hands under the tap. "You know how much I hate vacuuming."

"Too bad. That could have tipped the scales."

Changing tactics, he grabbed Gran's tea towel from the stove handle. "How about if you don't do it, you get this." He dried his hands and twirled the towel until it was tight, then snapped it in the air.

Her eyes went wide. "You wouldn't."

He took a step toward her, and she took one back, because she clearly knew he would. "Try me."

"Don't," she shrieked. "My ass is sore enough already." As soon as the words left her mouth—a sweet reminder of last night—they both stood stock still, the air between them charged. "I mean...uh..." she began, like she was trying to backtrack.

A warm flush crept up Sky's neck, and Matt tossed the towel onto the counter like it was on fire. Dexter finished eating and curled around his leg, giving him something else to focus on.

"Where are the plastic bags?" Sky asked, her voice a little hoarse. "I was going to do it all along. But now you have to make my bed for a week. Not that there is much to make," she rambled on. "It's been so hot in the bedroom lately, I only have one sheet on." She pulled the gloves on. "Is it hot in your bedroom too? I mean. Wait…"

Jesus, Matt had never seen her so flustered before. Coming to her rescue he grabbed the bag of litter by the door, and opened the closet where Gran kept the plastic bags stockpiled. At least fifty spilled out. Matt shook his head. He wasn't sure what her fascination with plastic bags was, but she could singlehandedly change the atmosphere and speed up global warming. "We'd better hurry. I don't want to miss morning visiting hours."

"Right." She nodded and followed him into the other room.

Changing subjects, he said, "I really hate Gran in this house alone."

He held the plastic bag open as Sky dumped the old litter into it. "Are you going to stay with her when she gets out?"

He nodded and tied the bag off. "I'll make arrangements for someone to be here in the day, but at night she'll need me."

Sky filled the box with fresh litter, and Dexter jumped right in and started pawing at it. "She'll like having you here."

He frowned, and while he wanted to help he hated being back in the house. It held nothing but bad memories. Sky touched his shoulder and he looked at her. "What?" he asked.

"Maybe you and Gran can make new memories. Good ones."

He shrugged. "Maybe."

"And maybe you could bring Murphy here to live with you. I'm sure he'd love that backyard."

He grinned, and gestured toward the three cats. "I'm sure they'd all get along."

"You never know until you try. Besides, Murphy is a big baby. They'd probably love him, and he could stay here and watch over Gran at night, and in the day the animals could all chase the birds together."

Matt smiled. "That would be his dream job."

"That's what this house needs," Sky said. "A dog, a happy couple and a houseful of kids to keep watch over Gran."

He laughed. "I know she'd love that. She's lonely here and I hate seeing her like that."

She went quiet, thoughtful for a moment, then crinkled her nose and asked, "What's going to happen to Murphy if you can't train him?"

He shook his head, not wanting to think about it. "Not too many people wanting to adopt a full-grown dog who loves to chase birds."

Matt tossed the bag into the kitchen trash and they washed their hands before walking through the house to check on it. It wasn't a big place, but it had good bones and a decent backyard. He stopped in Gran's room and looked at the floral bedspread. There was a time his mom and dad were happy, when they used to laugh in this very room, but then his mom got sick and died and his father started drinking. His heart squeezed when he thought of his mom. She'd made this house a home and filled it with love and laughter.

Sky was right. A dog, kids and a loving couple was exactly what this house needed. He put himself in that situation for a moment, and knew that's what it would take to help demolish all his bad memories. But Matt wouldn't be the one to give it what it needed, since the girl he loved was in love with another man.

"You okay?" Sky asked, her hand going to his back.

"Yeah, we should get going."

They made their way back to the front door and before Matt locked up, Sky grabbed Gran's knitting bag from beside her favorite chair. Traffic was light as they drove to the hospital. Sky parked and they both went inside to the nursing station, where they were guided to his Gran's room.

She was sleeping quietly as they entered, but woke when he stepped up to her bed. "I didn't mean to wake you," he whispered.

"Nonsense," she muttered, still a bit groggy from the medication. Her glance left his and went to Sky's. "Sky," she said. "You brought my knitting." She pressed her fingers together in front of her face. "You're a darling."

"How are you feeling?" Sky asked. When Matt started to fix Gran's sheet she shooed his hand away.

"Stop fussing," she said, and he was happy that the meds were keeping her pain-free, if not a bit loopy. "I'm just fine. Or at least I will be once I get out of here." Frail hands gestured to the tray on her nightstand, not a crumb left on the plate. "If they don't kill me with what they're trying to pass off as food first." She pulled her knitting needles and yarn from her bag, and the smile was back on her face as she slowly sorted out her supplies. There was real concern on her face when she asked, "How are my cats?"

"Just fine," Matt said.

She looked at Matt and blinked over her milky eyes. An arthritic hand reached out and closed over his. "I don't want to impose, Matt. But is there any chance you just keep an eye on them until I'm home?"

"Of course, you don't even have to ask, and when you get

out of here, I plan to stay with you until you're back on your feet."

"You're a good boy, Matt," she said her voice fading a little, then she looked down. Matt swallowed the lump pushing into his throat, because he knew what she was thinking. Knew she blamed herself for not being there when he was a kid. But it wasn't her fault; she'd been grieving for a lost daughter and had no idea how bad things had turned between Matt and his dad. "I can't ask you to do that," she said softly, understanding what the house meant to him, and the demons that still haunted him.

"You're not asking," he said, holding her bony hand between both of his.

Gran looked at Sky and her voice wobbled slightly when she said, "He's a good boy."

"I know," Sky said. "He's been my best friend since I taught him how to climb a tree."

"Hey," Matt shot back, and let Gran's hands go. "That's not how I remember it."

"Look at that, haven't even hit thirty yet and your memory is failing you."

Reaching for her knitting needles, Gran chuckled softly, then she went quiet like she was searching her memory banks. "That's right, your birthday is next Saturday. Do you have plans?"

"I plan to have dinner with the prettiest girl I know."

Gran's eyes opened wide, well, as wide as possible in her drug-induced state, and she looked at Sky. "Oh, is there something I should know?"

A warm flush of embarrassment came over Sky's face and he could only imagine she was reliving what they'd done last night. "I'm talking about you, Gran," he said, even though he knew Sky was the most beautiful woman he knew.

"Now, come on. You don't need to be fussing with me."

"There isn't a girl I'd rather spend it with," he said and that brought a big smile to her face.

"I might still be in this horrid place, and believe me, you don't want to eat what they're cooking."

Both Sky and Matt laughed. "If you're here, I'll bring the food."

"Don't be fussing," she said again. "You must have plans with Caleb. Didn't you all go to the cottage to celebrate his thirtieth?"

"Yeah, but I'll go down after dinner with you."

Kat, who worked at the hospital and knew about his grandma—news spread fast in their circle—poked her head in. "Hey, how is everyone doing?"

Sky waved her in and introduced her to Gran. After pleasantries were exchanged, Matt spoke quietly to Gran and Kat pulled Sky aside to say something to her. A few minutes later she stepped back up to him and put her hand on Matt's shoulder. He closed his hand over hers and tried not to react. But she felt so warm and familiar, it was doing the worst things to his insides.

"I'm going to leave you two alone to speak to Gran, okay?"

He gave her hand a squeeze. "You don't have to do that."

She gestured with a nod toward Kat, who was standing at the door, looking rather antsy. "Kat seems eager to show me something."

"Let me guess," he whispered. "Thor?"

Sky chuckled. "I think so."

"Okay, come find me when you're done."

She said her goodbyes to Gran, and he stayed with her for a little while longer. He was happy to see she was bouncing back so quickly. After visiting hours, he spoke to the doctor to find out that because of her age, they'd be keeping her for observation for at least a week. Matt gathered the informa-

tion they needed on home care, and he fired off a text to Sky
to meet him on the main level.

"Hey," he said when she stepped off the elevator.

"Everything good with Gran?"

"Yeah, I talked to the doctor and gathered some information. You all set?"

She nodded and he put his hand on the small of her back
to lead her out through the sliding main doors. They hopped
into her car and headed to the bar.

The lunch crowd started to pile in by the time they
arrived, and Sky went in back to put the food order in and
talk with her manager, Marco. Matt grabbed the pool balls
from behind the counter and made his way to the table. He
racked the balls and took a few shots, keeping himself occupied while they waited for the order. Sky leaned against the
bar talking to Marco and while he couldn't hear what they
were saying, from the look on her face, he could tell it was
serious.

Marco stepped into the kitchen and Matt walked the
length of the table. He bent to take a shot and caught Sky
from his peripheral vision. She was staring at him, his ass in
particular. He looked around to see who else was at the bar,
assuming she was pretending for someone else's benefit.
Either that or last night had changed something in her. *Yeah,
wishful thinking, dude.* He saw a few of his friends, but when he
looked back at the spot where she was standing, he found
it empty.

Passing it off as nothing more than Sky going into one of
her daydreams—probably plotting her next story, or her life
with Caleb, he finished sinking the balls, then went to the
kitchen to help her pack up the food.

She put the last of the sandwiches into a paper bag and
smiled up at him, but behind that smile he spotted something else. Was it unease? Was last night harder on her than

she was letting on. He cursed under his breath, angry with himself.

"All set," she said.

He grabbed the bag from her and carried it to her car. They climbed in and he turned to her. "You okay?"

"Yeah, why?"

"I can tell when something's bothering you, Sky. It's me, remember."

Her smile was slow. "Yeah, it's you," she said, her voice soft, like it was when they were between the sheets. When he spanked her. Fuck.

"I really am sorry. I—"

"Matt," she said cutting him off. "It's okay. I'm okay."

"You sure?"

She nodded and turned the engine over. "Now let's get these sandwiches delivered and get this breakup done and over with. I'm sure you're more than ready to be done with this ruse."

Is that what she thought? If so, she was way off base, but he wasn't about to tell her the only girl he wanted was her. Pushing down the lump climbing into his throat, he fiddled with the radio until he found his favorite station. He cranked the volume and for the most part silence hovered between them as they drove to the outskirts of town, to the old abandoned base where the guys were training dogs. He jumped from the car to open the gate and after Sky drove through he shut it behind them. When Murphy saw him, he came running over, a tennis ball in his mouth.

"Hey, Murph," Sky said, petting him on the head. She grabbed the ball and threw it, and the smile that lit up her face tugged at his heart. She was so sweet, with an innocent sensuality about her that filled him with possession.

He grabbed the bag of food from the car and looked at Caleb's SUV. Sky's eyes darted around nervously and her lids fluttered a little faster when she spotted Caleb coming toward them.

"Hey, how's Gran?" he asked when he stepped up to them.

Sky looked at Matt and they exchanged a long look. "I'll hand out the subs." She took the bag from Matt and walked away.

"What's up with Skywalker?" Caleb asked, shading the sun from his eyes, watching as Sky step into the compound.

"It's just not working out between us," Matt said.

"No?"

Murphy came back with the ball and Matt grabbed it. He gave it a good hard throw, sending it to the other side of the compound where Jack and Garrett were setting up the detonation boxes used for training.

"You know what?" He put his hand on Caleb's back. He hated lying to his friend, but when all was said and done and the two were living happily ever after in a house with a picket fence, they'd all be able to laugh at this. "We gave it a shot, but she's not the girl for me."

"Are you serious?" Caleb asked. "I thought you were...*smitten*."

Despite the storm going on inside him, Caleb channeling Gran put a smile on his face.

"No, we're just better as friends," he said.

Caleb stared at him.

Don't look away, dude. Don't do it.

He looked away.

Under the guise of searching for Murphy, he narrowed his eyes and glanced around the courtyard. "Where the hell did he go? He must have found a bird to chase."

Caleb stared at him a moment longer, then said, "So, she's free to date anyone she wants?"

Matt nodded. "Yeah, she is. And actually, I'm pretty sure

she was always more interested in exploring a relationship with you than me."

Caleb eyes widened with interest. "Really?"

"Yeah, really."

"Hmmm," Caleb said.

"What?"

"Nothing. I guess...I just...I had no idea."

Matt looked back at him. "I think you should ask her out. I think you two are better suited for each other."

Caleb laughed. "Better suited? Seriously, Matt? You're like a goddamn eighty-year-old woman."

Matt laughed. "Fuck off."

"I think you should be hanging out with Luke at Sheffield community center."

"Why's that?"

"That's where the retirement group hangs out. Any one of those ladies will snap you up." He paused to shake his head, his lips turning up at the corners. "No wonder it didn't work out with Sky." Caleb drove his thumb into his chest. "She needs a man who's up to speed."

"What part of fuck off didn't you get?"

Grinning, Caleb grabbed Matt and put him in a headlock. He ran his knuckles over Matt's head. "Hey come on, bro. You know I'm just fucking with ya."

Matt gave him a jab in the kidneys and Caleb let loose a breath and tackled him to the ground. They rolled around in the dry soil, creating cloud dusts that filled his mouth and eyes with dirt. Murphy and Oscar came running over, barking and nipping at their heels.

"You two need a room?" Jack asked, and they both blinked up to see their friend looking over at them.

Laughing and rubbing the debris from his eyes, Caleb jumped up and held a hand out to Matt. He pulled him to his feet and when they were standing eye to eye, Caleb said, "So you really think I should ask her out?"

Putting on his best poker face, he answered with, "Yeah, I do."

"Dude, you sure about this? You know I'd never cut in where I don't belong."

Jack's glance left Matt's to go to Caleb's "What's going on? Who are you asking out?" he asked, never one to let anything get by him.

Caleb wiped the dirt from his pants. "Sky. Matt said they decided they were better as friends." Sky came from around the corner of the compound, and Caleb put his hand on Matt's shoulder. He gave a squeeze and said, "I'll catch up with you later."

Jack eyed him, and Matt tried not to fidget under his scrutiny. "Is that right?" he asked. "There's nothing more between you and Sky?"

"That's right," Matt said, meeting and holding Jack's gaze, despite the man being an expert at reading others. "It was a crush. I'm over it."

Jack made a throaty noise—the kind that called a guy out on his bullshit without ever having to open his mouth. "So I guess I can ask her out now," Jack said.

Selfish bastard that he was, the thoughts of Sky with anyone other than him filled him with rage.

Don't flinch dude. Don't flinch.

He flinched.

Matt's focus went to Caleb, who'd darted across the compound to catch up with Sky. He playfully tugged on her hair and she blinked up at him. Matt didn't have to be in hearing distance to know his best bud was in the middle of asking the girl Matt was in love with out on a date. Sky's glance went from Caleb to Matt and held for an extra moment. Air evacuated his lungs in a whoosh. He planted his feet and balled his hands. Jesus, it was all he could do to keep himself from crossing the compound, pulling her into his arms and claiming her as his own.

Play it cool, Matt. This is what she wants.

"Yeah, it's really easy to tell you're over it," Jack said.

9

"So it worked then," Kat said, a smug grin on her face. "I told you it would. Every guy wants what another guy has."

"You were right," Sky said. "Matt and I," she paused to do air quotes around the words, "'faked a breakup' at the compound this morning and then Caleb asked me out to dinner. He said he hasn't seen enough of me lately and just wanted a quiet meal with the two of us."

"But it's a date, right?"

"I think." Actually, she wasn't even sure. "We're going out this Friday night."

"Then why do you look so...to quote Gran...mopey? This is what you want, right? What you've wanted all along."

Sky's gaze went to Matt, and she leaned against the countertop as sweet memories rushed through her thoughts. Honest to God, she didn't know what she wanted anymore. A noise caught in her throat as she studied him. They really had gone from zero to one hundred in record time. Or had they? They'd always been close, always touched, laughed and carried on like two people who had feelings for one another. It wasn't until he kissed her that she realized just how deeply hers ran. Maybe they were already registering on the needle before she'd fallen into bed with him. Warmth spread through her, and she exhaled a fluttery breath as her mind once again went back to his bed.

"What's gotten into you?" Kat asked as she sipped on her drink and spun back and forth on her stool like an antsy five-year-old. "Hello. Earth to Sky," Kat said, waving her hand in front of Sky's face.

"Ah...what?" Sky said, dragging her focus from Matt—his ass specifically—as he bent over the pool table, cue stick aimed. She met her friend's glance and took in her raised eyebrows as her gaze moved over Sky's face. "What?" Sky asked again, struggling to keep her mind on her conversation with Kat and off Matt's backside—and what they'd done the night before. "So Thor's pretty hot," she said, striving to shift Kat's focus off the dreamy look she knew was on her face, and onto Kat's sex life. "I can see why you like him. I guess you don't find guys like him in Mississippi. I don't blame you for wanting to move here. Closer to Tallulah, and you're right, the men are a lot hotter."

Dear God, she needed to stop rambling or she was going to give herself away.

Kat's eyes went saucer-wide and she stopped spinning to plant both palms flat on the counter top.

Too late.

She lifted herself up a bit, and leaned toward Sky. "Oh. My. God," she said, drawing each word out slowly.

"What?" Sky asked again, grabbing the dishcloth to wipe down the already spotless oak bar top. Even though it was sterile, she needed to busy her hands before they got her into more trouble. Because as she looked at Matt, all she could think about was going over there and reacquainting herself with his hard body. Her hands tingled as she thought about it. So did another body part.

Get it together, Sky.

Easier said then done, because how could she possibly think of anything else but what went on his bed late last night. He was so wild, intense...possessive. Everything Kat had said about him was true. He was a take-charge guy in the bedroom, one who liked to hold his girl down and take her hard. And those spankings.

Oh, my God, those spankings.

She could feel heat rush to her face as she thought about the way he'd flipped her over, only to give her backside a good hard slap. How could she possibly go back to vanilla sex after experiencing Matt's brand of lovemaking?

"What's going on?" Tallulah asked when she came back from the bathroom. "Sky, are you okay? You look...flushed."

"That's because she had sex," Kat stated matter-of-factly.

"What?" Tallulah said, her voice rising. "You and Caleb had sex? When did this happen? He only just asked you out this morning, didn't he?" She paused and tapped the bar. "You've been here working since you left the compound this morning. When did you have time?"

"We didn't have sex," Sky explained.

"So then..." Kat frowned and looked down and Sky could almost hear the wheels spinning. A few beats later her eyes lifted and her head jerked back with a start. "You had sex with Matt," she blurted out so loudly a few customers at the table behind them all turned her way. "I should have guessed. I saw the way you two were acting with each other today when I ran into you at the hospital. And you were flushed. I thought it was because the hospital was so damn hot, but now I know what was really going on."

"Shh," Sky said, whacking Kat with the cloth. "Everyone can hear you."

"Don't shush me," Kat said.

"And Matt and I weren't acting any differently." That much was true. They'd always touched a lot. "And I was flushed because it *was* hot at the hospital. They keep Gran's room warm for her. They do that with the elderly."

Ignoring her explanation, Kat held her palm toward the ceiling and waved her fingers toward herself. "I want all the details. So spill."

Sky turned to Tallulah, whose jaw was practically hitting the bar top. Grabbing a glass, Sky poured a soda, dropped a straw into it, and pushed it toward her. "Here. Drink this."

Tallulah took a long pull from the straw and then said, "Okay, what the hell is going on?"

"I don't know," Sky said, burying her face in her hands. "It just...happened."

"Sex doesn't just happen, my friend," Kat said. "Not without two people wanting it to happen."

"We'd come from the hospital, he was upset, and he reached out to me, that's all."

"I told you he liked you," Kat said.

She thought about the regret on his face come morning. "He doesn't like me, Kat. Not like that."

"Did he get hard?" Kat bobbed her head in an "I told you so" sort of way.

"Yeah, but he's a guy in his twenties," Tallulah piped in. "A good stiff wind could make him hard."

"That's true," Kat said. "And he's been holed up at the bar studying forever and hasn't been with anyone lately."

"But still, he must like her, right?" Tallulah toyed with her straw. "Otherwise he wouldn't have slept with her."

Kat nodded. "My thoughts exactly."

As her friends discussed her and Matt's sex life, Sky poured herself a soda and took a big drink. When she was done, she put her glass back down on the counter harder than was necessary. But it did the trick because both girls stopped talking and turned to stare at Sky.

"Are you two done discussing my sex life?"

"Not at all. We want to hear everything," Kat said. "Did he...was he...you know. Crazy kinky?"

Sky tried not to show a reaction, but her mind instantly rewound to last night. Her toes curled as fire licked over her thighs. Her hand went to her backside, and she rubbed gently. Something told her he'd barely scratched the surface with her, and had a lot more kink up his sleeve. Damned if she didn't want to find out.

"He was that good, huh?" Tallulah asked.

Kat let loose a long slow whistle. "I am so damn jealous. Next time—"

"There's not going to be a next time. It was an accident. A one-time thing. Matt even apologized when we woke up. He told me he wasn't in his right mind."

"Yeah, probably because he knows you're crazy about Caleb," Tallulah said.

"Which you still are, right?" Kat asked. "Or did a night with Matt rock your world so hard it shook some sense into you."

"What's that supposed to mean?"

"It means, Caleb is hot and everything. But Matt...well, Matt is the whole package."

"So you said."

"You disagree?"

Her head lifted and from across the room she watched Matt work the pool cue. He chalked the end and slid it along those big hands of his. Her mind instantly revisited the way he took his cock into his hands and stroked it before sheathing himself. Her breath came out a little fluttery, her heart pounding just a little faster.

"Yes... No... I don't know."

"Then tell me what you do know. Did he hold you down hard and give it to you good?"

A sound squeaked in her throat. "Yes," she managed to get out, even though she wasn't one to kiss and tell.

Kat raised her hands in the air like she was celebrating her favorite team's touchdown. "I knew it!" she yelled.

"It might have been great, Kat, but it's not going to happen again."

"Why the hell not?"

"It was...it was," she began, struggling to explain it. "Like a reaction. You know, when two people experience something traumatic, or find themselves in a stressful situation, they form an attachment and things...happen."

"Okay, so Matt was under stress because of Gran. That doesn't explain why *you* let it happen."

Wasn't that the question of the hour?

"I was under stress too," she said.

Kat pointed a finger at her. "What you were under, my dear friend, was Matt."

Kat and Tallulah laughed and high-fived each other.

"Oh my God, you two. Cut it out." She glanced up to see Matt staring at her, and felt a little breathless under his intense gaze. "Great. Now Matt probably knows what we're talking about."

"On that note," Tallulah said, glancing at her watch. "It's time for Garrett and me to head home."

"Give Lexi a kiss for me," Sky said.

"I better take off too. Thor has an early therapy appointment tomorrow, and we have a lot of *kinks* to work out."

Sky rolled her eyes. "You are bad."

"Because it's way more fun than being good. And if you want my advice, Sky..."

Sky held her hands up. "I don't."

Kat laughed. "Fine but I will say this. Don't blow a good

thing." She winked and added, "Or rather, go ahead and blow it."

Sky's eyes went wide, not because of Kat's horrible advice, but because Matt was standing behind her.

He gave Kat an odd look as she and Tallulah headed toward the door, then he turned his attention to Sky. "I'm going to run and check on Gran, then I'll be by to help you lock up. Wait for me, okay?"

There were only a few customers left, and while Sky could close up early and head home before he got back, she nodded, knowing better than to voice an argument. And truthfully, she liked him walking her home, especially after the incident with Simon.

She watched him leave. Once he was gone, she swept behind the bar, then went over the books while she waited for the last of the patrons to leave. She thought about her conversation with Marco earlier that day. He wanted to buy into the business, and had presented her with a new business plan. She sat on her stool and considered it for a time as she nursed a soda. Her mind went back to what Matt had said about freeing up her time for other things in her life, and how her father would have wanted that. Her heart pinched as she thought of her dad.

She grabbed Marco's proposal from beneath the counter and studied the numbers. His investment and new marketing plan would really breathe new life into the place, and if he was more involved, she could go back to school and take the classes she always wanted to.

Her head waitress Amber came up to her and pulled her thoughts back. She put her tray on the counter and said, "Quitting time."

Sky smiled at her, then glanced around the empty lounge. "I'll walk you out." She followed Amber to the door and stood there until she was in her car. Once she was gone, Sky locked up and walked to her office, where she booted up her laptop. She opened the book she was working on and began reading through the last few pages she'd written.

Soon enough she found herself daydreaming, staring at the pages as the book played out in her mind's eye. Only problem was she was suddenly visualizing Matt as the hero, and not Caleb.

Oh boy.

She closed the laptop and stole a glance at her watch. Visiting hours were over long ago, and Matt should have been back by now. A loud noise sounded outside in the back parking lot, and unease swept through her. She grabbed her bat from beneath the counter and hurried to the back door.

Unlocking it and inching it open slowly, she peered into the night, and what she saw had her heart leaping into her throat, and her blood draining to her toes.

———

Matt turned to see the shock on Sky's face. "Get back inside and lock the door," he yelled.

Sky stood there staring, her face going white as her glance left his to go to Simon's, whose face was still bruised from his last beating. He held Matt's arms from behind as the mouth breather used Matt's stomach as a punching bag.

Simon laughed. "Don't worry, sweet thing. When we're finished with lover boy here, it will be your turn. And if you're real nice, I'll be real nice too."

"Sky. Go. Now," Matt said before another hard fist hit his gut. Air left his lungs in a whoosh, and he bent forward, only for Simon to pull him to a standing position again. He spit blood, but before he could break free, the Neanderthal turned his attention to Sky and started toward the open door.

Sky was in danger.

That thought filled Matt with rage. Adrenaline pumped through him and he threw his head back, catching Simon in the face. The sound of bones crunching punctured the quiet night and the curses that followed were a good indication that he'd broken the asshole's nose. But he didn't have time to check, not with Simon's goon about to reach Sky.

He broke from Simon's hold and dove for the other guy, catching him around the waist. He dragged him to the ground, and felt a fist to his side as he struggled to gain purchase. They rolled on the asphalt, until Matt was on top. He pinned the man's arms with his knees and started pummeling the guy's face, driving his head into the unforgiving pavement.

Some small part of him registered that Sky was still standing there, bat poised and ready for battle. But his thoughts blurred when something shattered over his skull. Sky screamed with the sound of breaking glass and moved toward him. He turned to see Simon holding a broken bottle out like a weapon, but then the bat swatted across his hand and it smashed to the ground.

Simon yelled and held his busted arm. He dropped to his knees, curses filling the back parking lot. Matt jumped off the guy groaning beneath him and grabbed Sky. Breathless as his mind raced to catch up, he dragged her inside and locked the door behind them.

He pushed her up against the wall and looked her over. "Are you okay?"

She nodded, her eyes wide, full of fear. "He was going to kill you. I thought...I was so...so scared."

"Wouldn't have happened. I would have taken it from him." A broken bottle was nothing compared to what he'd been up against overseas.

Her finger went to the blood on his lip, and her voice wavered when she said, "They hurt you."

"It's okay. I'm okay," he said. But as he looked at her pallor, he knew she wasn't. "Let's call Garrett and get you home."

He led her to her office and she fell into the chair. Matt reached for her phone and by the time Garrett arrived, Simon and his muscle were long gone. They gave their statement and Garrett left to go hunt them down. He put his arm around Sky and stepped outside. She looked around nervously, and he cursed under his breath. He'd promised to keep her safe from that asshole Simon, only for this to happen.

"Don't worry," he said. "I'm sure Garrett has them in custody by now, and we'll get a restraining order first thing tomorrow. I don't plan to let you out of my sight until this matter is dealt with."

He wanted to get her home quickly, but since she wasn't a fan of riding on the back of his bike, he left it in the parking lot. He grabbed his helmet in one hand and pulled her against him with the other. A quake moved through her, and he pulled her in tighter to offer his comfort.

They hurried along the dark sidewalks and he pointed to the sky, trying to lighten her mood. "There's Venus," he said.

She gave him a shove, a small smile on her face when she countered with his juvenile response, "Where's Uranus?"

Matt laughed, and when they reached their building, he opened the security door and led her up the stairs to her apartment. He ushered her inside and locked the door behind them.

He put his helmet down. "Why don't you go get changed and I'll make some tea."

He swiped his tongue over the cut on his lips and all the humor was gone from her eyes as she looked over his face. "I think we should get you cleaned up first." Grabbing his hand, she gave a little tug to lead him down the hall. He moved with her, his stomach muscles taking that moment to ache from the pounding.

He grunted, and she darted a quick glance behind her, worry washing over her face. They reached the bathroom and he took a look at himself in the mirror. Blood crusted beneath his right eye, and he could already see purple bruising.

"I'll clean this up, then you can take a shower." Sky gestured for him to sit on the edge of the tub, and when he lowered himself, she leaned over him to turn the water on. Her stomach pressed against this shoulder, and he fought the urge to pull her onto his lap, wrap his hands around her and keep her with him forever.

She adjusted the nozzle then walked to the sink as he tugged his bloody shirt over his shoulders. Pulling open the medicine cabinet mirror, she rooted around inside and came back to him with cotton balls and antiseptic. She knelt down in front of him, and his heart began to pound harder against his chest.

Her hand went to his face as she ran the cotton over his cut. Everything from her nearness to the scent of her skin, to the way her hair brushed against his shoulders, made him breathless. Fighting for a measure of control, he clenched down hard on his jaw, but she mistook the reaction for pain, and for that he was grateful. They'd already crossed a line once, and he had no intention of doing it again.

"Sorry. I know this stings a bit. I'm almost done." She dabbed his cheek a few more times, then dropped the cotton ball into the trash. When she turned back to him, a warm palm touched his cheek, her gaze moving over his cuts. "All cleaned," she said.

Even though everything inside him was telling him to walk away, to step outside and clear his head, he closed his hand over hers and leaned into it, needing her touch almost more than he needed to breathe. His heart raced and he strived for normal, but she was so warm and sweet, and the way she'd come to his rescue with the bat... A strong surge of protectiveness raced through him. If anything had happened to her tonight... He briefly closed his eyes, but when he heard her intake of breath, he opened them to find her staring at him.

He forced a smile. "My little slugger. I owe you a thanks."

"I think I owe you a bigger one."

His stomach twisted, knowing tonight could have gone down so differently. "Sky, if anything ever happens like that again, and I swear to God, it had better not, promise me you'll get yourself somewhere safe, okay?"

She swallowed hard, clearly shaken by tonight's events. "Matt," she murmured, moisture gathering in her eyes.

"Sky," he whispered, and brushed her hair from her face. "I'm serious."

She leaned into him, her breath warm on his neck as she shuffled closer and wrapped her arms around him.

"Hey," he said, cupping the sides of her head and inching back a bit so he could see her. "Are you okay?"

He watched her swallow, and his heart squeezed at the concern in her eyes—concern for him. "I was scared," she choked out. "I thought I was going to lose you."

As soon as the words left her mouth, his heart raced. He'd been scared tonight too. Not for himself, but for her. She was everything to him, and if those assholes had gotten their hands on her...if they'd laid one tiny finger on her... A violent tremble moved through his body.

"Matt, those guys..." she asked.

"I know." He exhaled sharply and closed his eyes in distress. "If anyone ever hurts you, Sky..." He let his voice fall off, not wanting to frighten or worry her any more than she was, but the truth was if anyone ever so much as touched a hair on her head he would kill them. He'd beat their fucking heads into the pavement until they were dead. The thought was primal, he knew, but he couldn't stand the idea of anything bad happening to her.

He pressed his forehead to hers and sucked in a couple of quick breaths. "I don't want to lose you," he murmured, his emotions a hot fucking mess. He dragged her into his arms and angled his head until his mouth was right there, inches from hers. "I can't lose you," he murmured, the love he felt for her engulfing him and weakening his resolve. "I just can't."

Her hands went to his shoulders and she ran the soft pads of her fingers over his flesh, derailing his ability to think. His pulse skyrocketed because there was nothing impersonal in the way she was touching him. In fact, it was sensuous and deeply intimate. Need pumped through his veins and before he even knew what he was doing his lips were on hers, kissing her hard, desperate to lay claim.

Her hands slipped past his shoulders to slide down his back. A soft moan caught in her throat and that was all the prompting he needed. He stood, dragging her up with him, and their eyes met as he pulled her shirt from her pants. He watched her chest rise and fall as he peeled it over her shoulders. Heat arced between them as hot steam filled the air. He slipped his hand around her back and released the clasp on her bra. It fell to the floor, and a tortured moan cut through the air as he reached out to brush the undersides of her breasts.

"So beautiful," he whispered as a fire igniting inside him.

"Matt," she murmured, her voice as shaky as her body. He took in the flurry of conflicting emotions passing over her eyes and pulled his hand back, some small, coherent brain cell warning him to stop this before they got in over their heads again. But the warmth of her skin was calling out to him, doing mind-fucking things to his body. She made a soft, sexy noise, and placed her hand on his chest. She splayed her fingers and let them drift down, running them over his chest, his stomach, the top of his jeans. His muscles rippled when she went lower still, to cup his throbbing cock through his pants. Fuck. He took a deep breath and tried to get his shit together as she gently massaged him, his dick growing thicker under her touch.

"Sky..." he growled, and tugged her hair, working to rein in his need for her. Jesus, they shouldn't be doing this, not again. It was clearly a reaction to tonight's events and if he knew what was good for him—and her—he'd put a stop to this once and for all. "We're both upset," he said, a frantic edge to his voice as she emotionally and physically reached out to him. "We shouldn't be doing this."

They exchanged a long look, and as primitive need raged inside him, he moved against her hand, his actions contradicting his words. But how could he possibly stop himself, when being with her like this felt so right?

"I need you to tonight, Matt," she whispered, her voice so soft, so damn inviting as she rubbed him harder, letting him know in no uncertain terms that she needed the physical connection. Flames licked a path up his thighs as she pressed against him. When she made another sexy noise, and he caught the heat in her eyes, he opened his mouth, desperate to put a measure of distance between them. He gripped her shoulders, needing this to end as much as he needed to continue it.

"Sky," he murmured, about to push her away. But her bare breasts felt so good against his chest, and when her mouth went to his neck, his words of protest were lost on a groan. Shivers of pleasure raced through him and he closed his eyes in surrender. Utterly trumped and fighting the inevitable, he shut out the clanging bells in his head, blocking all rational thought as he let need take over. Tomorrow he'd deal with the consequences and find a way to keep his distance, but right now, well, right now if he didn't touch her and taste her, he was sure he'd blow like a round of C4.

With common sense kicked to the curb, emotions and sensations ripped through him. She must have felt the shift in him because she abandoned his neck, her mouth going to his chest. Jesus, her lips felt like fire on his skin.

Her lips teased over his flesh, her tongue circling his nipples, coming perilously close with each swirl. He ran his hands through her hair, holding her to him, but they fell to his sides when she broke free and stepped back. Her gaze never left his as she shed her pants and panties, moving with a sensuality that damn near killed him. Desire slammed into him as she tossed her clothes away and stood before him fully naked, his for the taking.

He stared at her, finding it most difficult to take his gaze off her beautiful body and the way she was offering it up to him. "Sky," he whispered, the love he felt for her coming over him, blindsiding him and leaving him feeling like he'd been sucker punched. Tonight's beating was nothing compared to what he felt now.

His heart squeezed as he watched her, not daring to move...breathe. He stood there motionless as she reached out to him, her fingers going to the button on his jeans. Her chest rose and fell with a deep intake of breath, the heat of her mouth fanning out over his bare flesh.

With a hungry look in her eyes, she popped the button and pulled his zipper down. His pants fell to the floor, and she stared blatantly at his cock as it strained against his boxers and clamored for attention. He looked down, and when he saw the moisture on his skin, it reminded him of the fight. He tore the rest of his clothes off, climbed into the hot shower and pulled her in with him.

With the spray on his back, she grabbed the soap from

the rack and lathered her hands. His cock thickened when she touched him, running her soapy hands gently over his chest. He threw his head back and groaned when her hand dipped lower, wrapping around his girth. She squeezed and ran her hand along his length. His cock pulsed in her palms and she made another sexy noise that filled him with longing.

"Sky," he murmured, his throat so tight it was hard to talk.

Shutting out everything except the woman touching his body and the things she made him feel, his mouth settled possessively over hers. She moaned and moved beneath him, matching him kiss for kiss, touch for touch. His tongue tangling with hers as he raced his hands over her body, both of them stroking each other with aroused eagerness. Hot water fell over them, soothing his aching muscles and washing the soap from his skin as he took the bar from her. He ran it over her body, soaping her breasts, her stomach, between her legs. With his blood pulsing hot he set the bar aside and put his fingers back between her legs.

He touched her clit, and groaned when he felt how swollen she was. He applied pressure and Sky moaned and pushed against his hand. Her lashes fluttered, and she caught her bottom lip between her teeth. Body thrumming and entirely lost in the moment, he put his arms around her and picked her up, desperate for so much more.

"I need to be inside you," he growled, his breath coming in jagged bursts.

"Yes," she moaned. "Please..."

"Condom."

Her wet hair fell into her eyes when she shook her head. "I'm on the pill."

"I'm clean, Sky."

"I know that," she said.

The logical part of him couldn't believe he was doing this again, yet there was another part, an irrational part that couldn't wait to get his cock back inside her, to feel her squeeze him tight—to come for him. Jesus, what he'd do to make her come again. Since it was that irrational part that was calling the shots, he backed her up until she was pressed against the wall, and with one quick thrust he drove into her. He looked at her face as he plunged deep, nailing her against the tub enclosure. Eyes wide, her well-kissed lips opened and formed an O but no sound came.

With passion and protectiveness hitting at the same time, he started to pull out. He forced himself to remember this was Sky. Sweet, kind Sky who deserved soft and slow from him, not hard and rough.

"I'm sorry—" he began.

"Harder," she said, moving her hips urgently as her hands knotting around his neck. "Fuck me harder, Matt." Her nipples scraped against his chest, and when he met her glance and saw the desire reflecting there, his entire world turned inside out.

"Are you sure, baby?" he growled.

"Yes, harder," she cried out, grinding her clit against his pelvis.

He thrust back into her, driving her against the wall. A tremor raced through him as her muscles squeezed his cock, and he knew he wasn't going to last long at this rate. Christ, he could already feel the tension of an impending orgasm.

His mouth captured hers and their tongues tangled and slashed, like neither could get enough. Breathing hard, and barely able to fill his lungs, he inched out, then powered his hips forward, driving impossibly deeper. Air ripped from his lungs as their bodies joined and collided.

"Yes," she cried out, her nails digging into his back as she shared in the urgency.

Her fingers scratched over his flesh, sure to leave a scar.

But he wanted her to mark him as much as he wanted to claim her as his.

Her mouth moved under his and as she made a sexy noise, the crescendo of their union taking them higher and higher. His heart pounded erratically. Never, ever in his life had sex felt this good, this right. He shifted slightly, for harder thrusts. Feeling crazed, out of control, he drove into her. They crashed so hard against the tub enclosure he was sure they were going to break through it.

"That's it," she said. "Just like that." Her eyes closed as she came. "Oh, God, yes, just like that."

Her muscles clenched and he strived to hang on as her liquid heat scorched him. His mouth watered, aching to taste her. No longer able to hold on as she climaxed, her sex squeezing his cock in delicious ways, he threw his head back and let go.

"Yes," she cried out when she felt him pulse inside.

His cock throbbed, and he let loose a growl as he depleted himself in her. Her hands tightened around his back and he took deep breaths, desperate to refill his lungs.

With his heart still crashing against his chest, he pulled back, and set her on the floor of the shower. Brushing her wet hair from her face, he watched the way her burning eyes left his to slowly track his body. Life surged into his cock once again.

Suddenly, needing to possess her, savor her, to have her at his mercy, he turned the water off and stepped from the shower. He wrapped her in a towel and tied one around his waist. She just stood there looking up at him, like she didn't know what came next. As the need to have her restrained beneath him—his to do with as he pleased—stole his ability to think with clarity he carried her into the bedroom and tossed her onto the bed. Her towel fell away and he took that moment to drink in her beautiful body. Heat zinged through him and it occurred to him he'd never been so crazed before, had never lost his grip on sanity, but everything about her tore at his control, and turned him into some wild animal needing to mate.

She reached for the blankets, but he grabbed her hand to stop her. Dark lashes blinked rapidly over questioning eyes.

As he took in the sexy woman sprawled on the bed, it took a great amount of effort to find his voice. "I'm not done with you," he managed to get out.

She visibly shivered, excitement flaring in her eyes. "Oh."

His hands went to the towel knotted at his waist. "Hands above your head."

She lifted her hands and gripped her headboard, her legs widening for him. Ah, Jesus. Lamplight glistened on her sex, and it was all he could do to keep his cool. He pulled the towel from his waist and twirled it until it was a long rope.

"Matt?" Her eyes went wide, and he couldn't help but grin. The last time he'd twisted a tea towel it was with the intentions of snapping her ass. He planned to do that again, of course, but it would be with his hands, not the towel.

"I'm going to tie your hands," he explained.

A gasp caught in her throat and he needed to make sure it was from excitement, not fear.

He touched her body, running the back of his knuckles down the length of her stomach. "Do you trust me?"

"Always."

"Then you're okay with me tying you up and taking you the way I want."

Another gasp, and then, "Yes."

He moved to the head of the bed and wrapped the towel around her hands, then secured them to the headboard. His hands went back to her breasts and he stoked lightly. Her lips parted and her throaty purr resonated through his body.

Aching to indulge in her sweetness, he bent down and his

lips found hers. He kissed her long and hard, until they were both left shaking. He broke the kiss and climbed between her legs. Her hips came off the bed, but he pressed his hand to her stomach, shoving her back down and stilling her.

His eyes went to her pussy and he parted her with his fingers. Fuck. So wet and ready for him again. His cock throbbed, demanding to be back inside, but first he needed to kiss her all over, to watch her writhe beneath him as he took her higher and higher. He needed to hear her scream out his name. Needed to make her as crazed as he was.

Her body was warm and wanting as he fell over her and drew one plump nipple into his mouth. She moved and whimpered beneath him as he clenched down hard. Her bud swelled in his mouth, and as he ran the soft blade of his tongue over it, savoring her sweetness, lust burst inside him. He angled his chin and saw the need on her face, as she tossed her head from side to side. As her body came alive beneath him he abandoned her breast and ran his tongue down her body. He shimmied lower and gripped her thighs to widen them.

With her pretty pink pussy spread open, so wet and ready as she offered herself up so nicely, he caught her aroused scent and a shudder moved through him. Everything from need, possession and basic elemental instinct raged inside him as he bent forward to swipe his tongue over her.

So sweet. So fucking sweet. Her flavor played along his taste buds and a moan crawled out of his throat as ripples of pleasure raced through his veins.

Her whimper lingered in the air as she quivered beneath his mouth and the headboard banged as she pulled on it. "More," she whispered, and he heard the need, the impatience in her voice.

"You like that, do you?" he asked, not nearly ready to take

her. He wanted to play with her first, take command of
her body.

She whimpered her response, and began panting as he
stretched her lips wider, opening her up to him even more.
Jesus he loved seeing her like this. Giving her more of what
she wanted he ran his tongue over her, licking from bottom
to top before pushing it in deep. She squirmed in response,
and with that he buried his face between her legs to kiss her
hungrily. Her breathing became faster as he sucked her
inflamed clit. She undulated against his mouth, her sexy
noises making him insane. Consumed by the hunger burning
though his blood, he dipped a finger inside her and felt her
whole body quake. She grew slicker and slicker with each
stroke and a fever rose in him as her wet heat fueled his lust.

He pumped, stoking the fire inside her as he worked her
inflamed clit, urging her on as he feasted. Acutely aware of
the way his cock was aching, pre-come pooling on his crown,
he grabbed the base and stroked, running his palm up and
down the long length of his shaft.

He lifted his head, nudging her clit with his chin and
caught her watching him, her eyes focused on the way he was
gripping and stroking his cock. He took in the unabashed
heat in her eyes, the color flushing her cheeks and asked,
"You like watching?" She nodded, and he stroked his cock
faster, dipping into the juice on his head to lubricate himself,
as he pushed another finger inside her sex.

He felt a small ripple and knew she was close, but he
wanted to see her face when she came. She gave a cry of
protest when he abandoned her sex and climbed back up her
body. But that cry was quickly replaced by a moan when he
settled himself over her, and rubbed his cock along the
crevice of her opening. His mouth crashed back down over
hers and he kissed her like a man starved for so much more.

Her legs squeezed his sides, and there was no denying

how well her body fit with his. As he pillaged her mouth, roughly drawing her tongue into his, she moved beneath him, trying to force his cock in deeper, but he had other ideas.

"I want you on top," he said, his voice so gravelly he hardly recognized it. He reached over her head and untied her hands. He gave them a light massage where the towel had been rubbing, then he went down on all fours. Still on his knees, he was about to lower himself on the mattress, but before he could, Sky took his cock into her mouth. Christ it felt good. Then, before he realized what was happening, she pushed him onto the bed, and ran her tongue along the length of him.

Sweet mother fuck.

Her tongue swirled around his head sending shockwaves through him. His hips jerked upward, driving himself deeper into her mouth. Her hand slipped lower to cup his balls and when her heat wrapped around them, he could feel them draw into his body, his orgasm so damn close. His body hummed with tension as her head bobbed up and down, up and down. He pulled her hair to the side so he would watch and wished he hadn't. Seeing her mouth wrapped around him took him to the edge far too fast and he knew he needed to put a stop to her kissing and touching him if he wanted to last.

"Come here," he whispered, grabbing her by the shoulders and dragging her off him. He tapped her legs. "Climb over me." Her hair fell over her shoulder as she threw one leg over his thighs to straddle him from above. His cock stood erect and she shifted forward, trying to lower herself on him, but he held her still, wanting to control the pace.

He grabbed her ass and pulled her onto his stomach. "Don't move," he said, reaching for the towel. With her eyes closed and her head at an angle, she rubbed her hot wet pussy on his abdomen, and he slapped her ass. "Stop it," he growled.

She gasped, her lids opening. The desire he caught there touched something deep inside him, and when she rotated her hips, stimulating her clit, he knew exactly what she was up to—what she wanted. With possession raging inside him, he slapped her ass again, a little harder this time. She might have left her mark on his back, but he damn well planned to leave his on her ass.

She moaned in pleasure and he lifted himself slightly. He breathed in her sweet scent as he went to work on tying her hands around her back. Her chest jutted forward, just the way he knew it would. He licked one nipple, then blew on it, and watched the way her body shuddered. Taking control of their play he gripped her hips and lifted her. Positioning his cock at her hot opening, he slowly guided her down. She whimpered and squirmed like she wanted him to spear her, but he held her tight, controlling every inch as he fed her his cock. He groaned as her tight muscles squeezed his dick, and bit down on the inside of his cheek.

"More," she cried out, her head falling back, making her look so fucking sexy. He looked between their bodies, and saw half of his length inside her. Needing to completely bury himself, he tightened his hold on her hips and pulled her down hard, sinking every inch inside her and filling her to the hilt.

"Oh God," she cried out.

The pleasure was so intense, his head began spinning, so he took a moment to breathe, to savor and enjoy the feel of her silky warmth squeezing his cock like a tight glove. As he lost himself in her sweetness, she began rocking against him, her actions conveying what she needed.

Bending at the waist, he drew one hard nipple into his mouth as his hands intertwined in her hair. He gave a rough tug, pulling her head back slightly, and her moan of pleasure told him so much about her and her needs. With his front teeth he clamped down on her pale nub, and his other hand reached out, temporarily freeing it from the towel. He slid his hand down it until he shackled her wrist.

"I like watching too," he said around a mouthful of nipple. He placed her index finger on her clit, and fell back against the pillow. Heat danced in her eyes, but he didn't miss the hesitation when she realized what he was suggesting. He looked at her and decided no way in hell was he going to let her go shy on him now. Encouraging her to let go completely, he slid his hand between their bodies and put his thumb over her finger. He began moving it back and forth, and her mouth fell open in ecstasy. He pressed harder, and after they established a rhythm, he removed his finger, to let her take over.

She continued to stroke herself, and it had to be the sexiest thing he'd ever seen. He thrust upward and she cried out. "That's it," he said through clenched teeth, struggling hard to hang on. She began moving faster, bucking against her finger, and he loved watching her come undone, loved seeing this side of her.

Her thighs hugged him and he gripped her hips, holding her as she rocked against him. His body tightened and his muscles trembled as he powered into her, his thrust becoming harder and faster as he chased an orgasm.

"Yes," she murmured, her finger working faster over her clit.

"That's enough," he said. He grabbed her hand and retied it behind her back. "My turn." He pressed his thumb to her clit and watched the way her breasts bounced as she rode him.

"Oh God, yes," she cried out and her pussy clenched hard. He growled and when he felt her hot release drip down his cock and onto his balls, pressure built, coming to a peak. He began trembling from head to toe, unable to hold on any longer. He pulsed and throbbed with the hot flow of release as she fell over him, her beautiful breasts pressing into his chest.

At the peak of his orgasm he wrapped his arms around her back. Their fingers linked, and he held her to him, fighting for a measure of control as he continued to shoot his seed into her. She stayed on top of him, her wet hair falling across his chest. Seconds turned into minutes, and when he could finally move again, he untied her hands and pulled out of her.

Looking warm and sated, she snuggled in next to him, and he wrapped them in a blanket. He ran his fingers over her arm, enjoying the feel of her next to him. The blood slowed in his veins as he listened to her breathe softly. His brain finally stopped spinning and he looked down at the woman in his arms. Sex with her was so good, so right. In fact everything with Sky was better. But come tomorrow he'd have to get his shit together and get her back on track. She'd reached out to him for physical comfort tonight, but he could never forget that her heart belonged to another.

She rested her head against his chest, her warm breath tickling his skin. He tamped down the tug of emotions and cursed himself for not keeping a better check on them. He knew what they were doing was wrong, and wasn't going to pretend they had a future together. What did he have to offer her besides a good time in bed, anyway? Then again, he planned to become a doctor someday and then he could give her the life she deserved.

If you want her, then do something about it, some inner voice urged.

But she wanted his best friend, not him, so how could he possibly do something about it.

Wouldn't it be worse if you never tried?

10

S ky woke to the sound of birds outside her window. She stretched and when she felt her sore muscles, everything that happened last night, from the fight with Simon to the incredible sex with Matt, came rushing back in a whoosh. She turned and when she saw the other side of the bed empty, her heart fell into her stomach.

Filled with unease, she swallowed the lump pushing into her throat and pulled the sheet around her. She climbed from the bed and looked at her clock, surprised to see that mid-morning was upon them already. She padded through the apartment, but Matt was nowhere to be found. Taking off after sex wasn't like him, but then again, what did she know? She'd slept with him twice and the last time was at his place, which meant he had no place to take off to, right? Still, none of this felt right.

She went to work on making coffee as she ran over the events of last night. She remembered the conflicted look on his face, the way he'd tried to push her away when she'd reached out to him, physically, needing his touch, his comfort to wash away the memory of the attack from Simon.

How could she have done that? How could she have fallen into bed with Matt again, especially after she'd asked him to help set her up with their best friend? She was acting like a cheap slut. Sky had no problem with women having many sexual partners, but what she was doing with two guys who were her best friends—two guys who were as tight as brothers—went well beyond that. No wonder Matt had tried to put a stop to it. But instead of walking away she went and told him she needed him, then grabbed his cock and proceeded to kiss his neck, his chest. Oh, God.

What have I done?

Feeling her blood drain to her feet, she climbed from her kitchen chair and went in search of her phone, wondering if he'd messaged her. When she saw that he had, she didn't know whether to laugh or cry.

Went to visit Gran and make arrangements. Garrett tracked Simon down last night and took him into custody.

She started texting back, then stopped, feeling the strain she'd put on their relationship. When they woke up in bed the first time, he said he wanted to forget about it, and have things go back to the way they were. She tried. She really did. Last night he said she was reacting to the events of the night, like he did last time. While that might have been true for him, it wasn't entirely true for her. Ever since his first touch, her thoughts were consumed with Matt, her body craving the feel of him inside her again. She gulped. Oh, this was bad. It was so bad. Talk about a plan backfiring.

She sent a quick text back. *Give Gran a kiss for me, and what a relief that Simon is in custody.*

She stared at her phone for a moment and could see that he started to text back and stopped. She dropped her phone on her kitchen table and glanced at the work schedule pinned to her fridge. Matt wasn't scheduled to work tonight, and she wondered if he'd still come by to sit at the end of the bar and study. She hoped so, because she needed to talk to him and clear the air.

But what would she say? She took a moment to consider her feelings. Ever since they shared a bed in the boathouse, had let Kat's assessment of him get in her head, something had shifted inside her. She started looking at him differently. Started examining the depth of her feelings for him. One thing was for certain, however, what she felt went well beyond brotherly love.

Her phone pinged and her fingers fumbled as she reached for it, nearly knocking it to the floor. She swiped her screen to read the message.

Heard what happened last night. Are you okay?

She reread the message from Kat and texted back. *I'm good. Simon is in custody.*

Tallulah and I are headed to yoga. Come with us.

While her body could use a little stretching after working muscles she didn't even know she had, she knew she had sex written all over her. Kat would surely call her on it and want an explanation. But what could she say when she herself had no idea what was going on with her? *Can't today. Work from noon until five, but thanks.*

She tossed her phone down and jumped in the shower. After rinsing Matt from her body she plunked herself down at her table and opened her laptop. Part of her deal with Matt was to work on her book, so she decided to do just that. Only problem was her mind kept drifting. Sure she'd always been a dreamer when writing, but today she was too keyed up to concentrate. Her mind went back to Matt, to her work, her future.

Her date with Caleb Friday night.

Good God, how could she go through with it after all the things she'd been doing with Matt? But how could she not. Caleb was a good guy, and just a few weeks ago she thought he was the perfect guy for her. Stable and kind. It occurred to her that Matt was those things too, and everything a girl could ask for in the bedroom. But where did she stand with him now? He had to be avoiding her. It was the only logical explanation. Any other day he would have asked her to go see Gran with him.

When noon hour approached, she slipped her shoes on, grabbed her purse and headed to the bar. Inside she found the kitchen staff prepping for the Sunday lunch crowd, and after saying hello, she tied on her apron. For the next few hours she worked the bar while Amber took orders at the table. Her glance kept straying to the far end of the counter, and disappointment settled heavy in her gut every time she found it empty.

She picked her phone up to check it, and thought about texting him, only to put it down again. How was she going to make this right between them, and what did right even mean? Going back to the way things were? Was it possible to do that after sleeping with him again?

"Everything okay?"

She glanced up to see Kat take a stool across from her. Sky plastered on a smile and put a coaster in front of her friend. "Sure. How are things with you?"

Kat reached out and grabbed her hand. "You sure? Your hand is shaking." Kat's eyes narrowed and moved over Sky's face in a careful assessment. "Simon won't be around again."

"I know. I'm fine, really." She looked down to mask her eyes, wishing she were a better liar.

"Thank God Matt was there," Kat said.

Sky grabbed a glass and filled it with soda. She placed it on the coaster and said, "I know, right?"

Kat reached for a menu and flipped it open. "I heard they gave him a good beating."

"He got a few good shots in on his own," she said, quickly coming to his defense.

"I'm sure he did. He's not about to let anything happen to you. Like I said before, he's protective and possessive of those he cares about." She turned toward his empty seat. "Speaking of Matt, where is he?"

"He went to check on Gran and make some arrangements."

"Visiting hours were over long ago. I'm surprised he's not back yet."

She gave a casual shrug. "He probably had to go check on the cats."

Kat sipped her soda. "Probably."

The back door slammed and Sky's entire body tensed. She sucked in a breath and turned, expecting to see Matt. When she saw Marco walking toward the kitchen to check on orders, she exhaled, but didn't miss the way Kat was watching her.

"So your date with Caleb. Where is he taking you?" Kat asked.

"I have no idea."

"You must be excited."

"I don't know. Maybe this is a mistake. Maybe I shouldn't—"

"You can't back out now, Sky." Sky glanced up and was certain she saw a sly smirk on her friend's face before she wiped it away. "I mean everyone thinks you two will be good together. Even Matt."

A knot tightened in her stomach at the reminder. Matt wanted to see her with Caleb—wanted to forget they'd slept together.

Before she could respond, Marco stepped up to the bar, and she was grateful for the distraction.

"I'll catch up with you later," Kat said, grabbing her soda

and making her way toward the pool table, where a few soldiers were setting up a game.

"The guys in the kitchen told me what happened. Are you okay?" Marco asked, his eyes full of concern.

As she took in his warm, fatherly smile, her rattled emotions got the better of her and she could feel tears pricking her eyes. "I'm okay."

He drew her in for a hug, then ushered her down the hall toward the private office. "I don't like you working the night shift alone."

"I have to work, Marco. I can't afford to hire more staff."

He gestured toward the plush chair. She sat and he slid a paper toward her. "I know you're tired of hearing this, Sky, but with my investment you can hire more people, and breathe new life into this place."

She sat there for a long moment, looking over his business plan. "You're right," she finally said.

His head came up with a start, obviously surprised by her response. For years now he's been trying to buy into the business, but she kept refusing. But maybe Matt was right, maybe this was what her father would have wanted her to do. This way she could free up her time to go back to school, start thinking about the family she wanted. Plus last night had scared her, and Matt wasn't always going to be around to come to her rescue—especially now that he seemed to be avoiding her.

"I think it's time to start making some changes," she said softly.

Marco nodded, a smile on his face. "You father would be proud of everything you've done, Sky, but you and I both know working the bar late at night is no place for a young lady."

"I'm not doing this because of Simon," she finally said.

"No?"

"I'm doing this because it's right for me and I think this is what Dad would have wanted." She thought about Matt and how he'd opened her eyes to that and tried to get her to see past the pain of her loss. Thought about how he remembered her dream and insisted she follow through. He was such a good guy. A great guy.

And now, well...she might have chased him from her life.

"You're right, your dad would have wanted it."

She climbed from her chair and gave Marco a hug. "Welcome, partner," she said.

When she glanced up she saw Matt in the doorway looking at her. Matt, who was trustworthy, smart...rock solid. The perfect combination of rough and tender. Her heart squeezed when he smiled at her.

"Did I just hear what I think I just heard?"

She nodded. "I'm partnering with Marco."

"Finally," he said, and while he would normally hug her, she noticed he was keeping a measure of distance. She took in the warm and caring look on his face, and knew it was his way of saying everything was okay between them. But deep in her gut she knew it wasn't. How could they possibly move on from last night, pretend it didn't happen?

"Finally what?" Caleb asked, coming up behind Matt. Matt inched back, letting Caleb into the office.

"Sky is partnering with Marco," Matt explained.

"Oh, yeah?" he said. "I didn't know you were looking for a partner."

"Now she'll have more time to pursue her other interests," Matt explained, his eyes meeting hers.

"Like what?" Caleb asked. He pretended to swing a bat. "Batting lessons?"

As her glance went from Matt to Caleb it occurred to her that Caleb had no idea the little pigtailed girl had dreams to be a writer. But Matt, well, Matt knew everything about the girl she was and the woman she'd become, and not only did he know her inside out, he was the one who encouraged her to go after what she wanted. Which begged the question, what exactly did she want?

Caleb drew her in for a hug. "Matt told me what happened. I'm glad you're okay, but Matt can take care of himself. Don't ever do anything like that again, okay?"

Her glance left Caleb's and went to Matt's. Something seemed to come over him when he saw her in Caleb's arms. The muscles along his jaw ticked, and his fingers curled into fists.

Testing him, she looked back at Caleb. "About Friday night..."

Caleb pushed her hair from her shoulder, then gave a little tug. "Seven, okay?"

Her glance moved to Matt, who stood as still as a stealth soldier. She waited a moment, giving him a chance to say something, do something, but he continued to stare at her, his mouth pinched tight, so she responded with, "Seven is great."

———

Matt spent the better part of the week visiting and making arrangements for Gran, grateful that he had something to keep him occupied and his mind off Sky. Due to her age, and the fact that she wasn't healing as quickly as the doctors would have liked, Gran wouldn't be getting out of the hospital for another week or so. But he'd brought his stuff over earlier this evening, moving in before he really needed to because he didn't want to be at his place tonight when Caleb picked Sky up, and he certainly didn't want to be there in the morning if Caleb decided to stay the night.

He walked through the old house, Dexter purring at his

feet. He thought back to when Caleb had hugged her in her office at Sky Bar, and Matt considered the look in her eyes when she brought up her date with Caleb. For a fleeting second he thought he spotted something else in her gaze when she looked at him, something that went deeper than friendship. But if she felt more for him, then why would she keep her date with Caleb?

Because he's the guy she really wants, dumbass.

As his gut tightened, he stepped outside, locked the door and jumped on his motorcycle. He drove toward his apartment, and when he saw Caleb's SUV parked outside he spun around and headed to the bar. He parked, and made his way inside. When he found Josh and Jack at the pool table, he joined them.

"Hey, what's up?" Jack asked, taking a swig from his beer and placing it on the edge of the table.

In a shit mood, Matt grabbed a pool cue. "Nothing, why?"

"Oh, maybe because you look like a lovesick puppy that has just been kicked."

"I'm not in the mood for your counseling tonight, Jack," he said.

Josh went to work on racking the balls, as Matt signaled the new waitress for a beer. He looked around and was surprised to see that after only one week, Marco and Sky had made significant changes in the place.

Jack put his hand on Matt's shoulder. "Wouldn't dream of counseling you, pal."

"Yeah, why's that?" Matt asked.

Instead of answering, he said, "Where's Sky?"

"She's out."

"With Caleb?"

He shrugged and chalked his cue stick. "I'm not his keeper."

"Tonight's the night they're going on their first date, isn't it?"

"Yeah, I guess."

"Shame it didn't work out with you two. I thought you and Sky made a great couple."

"I'm not the guy for her. Caleb is."

"How do you know that?"

"I just do."

Jack laughed. "That sneaky bastard got to her before I could ask her out." The waitress came with Matt's beer and he took a huge drink. "If it doesn't work out with them, I think I'll ask her out," Jack went on to say.

The thoughts of her with another man—with Caleb—had his blood boiling and possession racing through him. "Don't," he said through gritted teeth.

"Why the hell not?"

"Because...just don't."

Jack put his arm back on Matt's shoulder. "And that's why you don't need any of my counseling. You already know everything you need to know."

11

Sky sat across from Caleb at her favorite restaurant. She took a sip of wine and fell into easy conversation with him. It actually felt weird to be on a date with him after all this time, and especially because she couldn't stop thinking about Matt.

She'd wanted to cancel the date, but Kat had insisted she go, plus she didn't want to be discourteous to Caleb, which was the only reason she was siting across from him right now talking about work, the dogs at the compound, Gran's health and how Matt had moved into the old house to take care of her. He was also interested to hear about her writing and how she wanted to go back and take some creative writing classes. He was a great conversationalist and she truly enjoyed being with him—but he was no Matt. Soon the meal was cleared and the waitress came back with the dessert menu.

"Coffee?" Caleb asked.

"Tea," she said, realizing how little he knew about her. Matt would have automatically known what her favorite after-dinner drink was. Just like he knew how much she really wanted to write for a living. The more she thought about

Caleb and Matt the more she realized what a mistake tonight had been. She and Caleb were friends, good friends, but there could be no more between them. They finished their drinks and Caleb pushed from his chair.

He looked at his watch. "We still have time to catch the late show if you want."

She shook her head. "I think I'll call it a night. I work the early shift tomorrow."

"Okay," he said.

His hand went to the small of her back when she stood, and he kept it there as he led her out of the restaurant. They reached his vehicle and he pressed the unlock button as she circled to the passenger side. She hopped into the cab, and as he backed out of the parking lot she fussed with the radio stations. They listened to the music, both lost in their own thoughts as he drove her home. Once there he parked and climbed from the driver's side seat.

"It's okay." She released the latch on her seatbelt, and put her hand on his. "I can see myself in."

"What kind of a gentleman would I be if I didn't walk you to your door." He cringed. "Besides, if I didn't Matt would kick my ass."

That brought a smile to her face. Matt was protective and possessive and he really would kick Caleb's ass, despite the fact that they were best friends, but when it came to her, he went above and beyond the role of friendship. It took a pretend relationship to open her eyes to the kind of man he was. She pulled her key from her pocket and opened the front door. She was about to step in when Caleb stopped her.

"Sky?"

She turned to face him and found him standing close. Too close. Oh, God, she hoped he wasn't going to kiss her. Perhaps she should say something, explain how she felt about Matt. She owed him that much after taking her on a date.

And she couldn't forget that Matt had told him that she was interested in exploring a relationship with him.

"Yeah," she said softly, wondering how she could tell him without hurting his feelings or coming across as flighty.

"This was...nice."

"Yeah, it was nice," she said, truly meaning that. She loved Caleb...like a brother, and spending one-on-one time with him *was* nice. He leaned into her and she turned her head so his kiss landed on her cheek.

He looked confused for a moment, then he asked, "Will you be at the cottage next week for Matt's birthday?"

She nodded. "I wouldn't miss it." She grinned and added, "After what he did to me on my birthday, I owe him a spanking and a dollop of icing on the nose."

When she thought about spankings, and putting icing on his body, heat moved through her, and she coughed to hide her sudden arousal.

"Garrett works Saturday and can't make it so the guys are going down Friday night. I have rounds, so I'll be late." He touched her hair and in familiar Caleb fashion, gave a little tug. "I guess I'll see you Saturday then."

"Okay. Good night, Caleb."

"Night, Skywalker."

Sky made her way inside and stopped to listen outside Matt's door, not that she expected him to be home. Just then her phone pinged. She grabbed it from her purse, her heart racing and hoping it was Matt.

You're home early.

She texted Kat back. *I work in the morning.* What was she supposed to say? Oh, I went out with Caleb but now I think I'm crazy about Matt. Talk about a plan backfiring in her face.

Want some company?

She thought about it for a moment. Honestly, she really

did need someone to talk to. Not that Kat gave the best advice, but still, her emotions were in a hot mess, and Kat was a good listener. *Sure*, she texted back.

She let herself into her apartment and threw her purse onto her coffee table. Her gaze went to her stack of DVDs. With her mind racing back to her conversation with Kat, she dug out Jenny and Ving's wedding video. She stuck it into her player and fell onto her sofa. She smiled when she saw Jenny walking down the aisle with her brother Garrett, and when they reached the altar and the camera panned wide to take in Ving waiting for her, Matt at his side, Sky's heart lodged in her throat.

She'd never seen him look more handsome in his suit, the warmth in his eyes as he watched Jenny, doing the weirdest things to Sky's insides. For a moment she visualized Matt standing there awaiting for her, watching her walk toward him, the look in his eyes similar but different. She thought about that, yet couldn't quite put into words the way Matt looked at her. One thing was for certain, she'd never seen him look at anyone else the way he looked at her.

The sound of her bell ringing prompted her into action. She turned the television off and jumped from the sofa. "Come in," she yelled.

Kat let herself in, took one look at Sky and said, "Oh, honey."

Sky put her hands to her face and exhaled. "I'm in big trouble."

"I know, come on."

Kat led her to the kitchen and gestured for her to sit while she filled the kettle with water. Ten minutes later she sat across from her friend, sipping chamomile tea.

"So what are you going to do?" Kat asked.

"I don't know," she answered, wondering how she failed to see what had been right under her nose all this time.

"There's always that napkin plan," Kat said, grinning.

"This is serous, Kat," Sky said, even though she couldn't help but grin too.

Kat's hand closed over hers. "I know. And I also know you and Matt belong together. I think everyone but you two know that."

"Then why did you tell me to go out with Caleb? I don't get it."

Kat rolled her eyes. "Because unlike you, I know guys and what makes them react."

"What is that supposed to mean?"

"Matt is crazy about you. Of that, I'm certain. I wanted you to go out with Caleb so it would push his buttons and finally get him to do something about how he feels."

"He didn't do anything."

"That's because he cares so much about you." Kat reached across the table and squeezed her hand. "You asked him to help you get together with Caleb, right?"

"Yeah."

"So he believes it's Caleb you want, not him. Don't you see, Sky? He's sacrificing what he feels for your happiness."

"Oh, God," she said, thinking about the way they came together in the bedroom. Everything inside her said it was more than just earth-shattering sex. They had a connection, one that went deeper than anything she'd ever felt before.

"Do you really think so?" she asked over the rim of her cup.

Kat nodded. "I know so."

She took a sip and put her cup down on the table. "What do I do?"

"It's his birthday next week, isn't it?"

"Yeah."

"Then show Matt it's him you want, not Caleb."

"Oh, God. I never should have gone on that date."

"Of course you should have. How else would you have known it wasn't Caleb you're in love with?"

"What must he think though?"

"Just talk to him, Sky. If there was no sexual spark, Caleb would know too."

She nodded, thinking about how she'd turned her head on the kiss. "But he tried to kiss me."

"Maybe he wanted to see if it could ignite a spark. Did it?"

"I turned my head."

Kat smiled. "Then Caleb already knows where you two stand."

"I still need to talk to him."

"For sure, but right now you need to think about how you're going to show Matt he's the one you really want."

"How can I do that?"

"Let me just say, actions speak louder than words."

"Meaning?"

Kat gave her a look that suggested she was dense. "Do you really need me to tell you that?"

Sky thought about that for a moment. There was no denying that she'd fallen for Matt—a guy who was the total package. Everything about him felt right, in her head and in her heart. As she thought about what Kat was suggesting, a plan began to formulate in the back of her mind. She gave it further consideration and as she began to warm to the idea, she couldn't help but smile. This Saturday was his thirtieth birthday. He might be having dinner with Gran before he headed down to the cottage, but once there he was definitely going to be having dessert with her. Oh, yeah, his thirtieth was going to be a night neither of them would forget in a hurry.

12

Matt stretched his legs out and twisted the cap off his beer, happy to just kick back and shoot the shit with the guys for a change and self medicate with a six pack—which was disappearing rather fast. He looked at Cole, Brad, Luke, Garrett, Ving, Josh and Jack as they all sat around the fire. The guys weren't just his comrades; they were his friends, there for the good times as well as the bad. The only one missing from the group was Caleb. His closet friend in the world, next to Sky.

Matt took a look at the late hour, grabbed his phone and sent him a text. *Where are you?*

Sorry, running late at the hospital. Not sure what time I'll get out of here.

Dibs on your bed. His reasons for not wanting to sleep on the boat were twofold. One, it was uncomfortable, and two, it reminded him of Sky and the way she'd snuggled in with him last time they were all at the cottage.

Fuck you, came Caleb's response.

Hey, it's my birthday.

Fine. I probably won't be in until late so I'll crash on the boat.

He powered down his phone and his thoughts returned to Sky as he tossed another log on the fire. He hadn't seen much of her after her date with Caleb, partly because he'd moved into Gran's place, and partly because they'd both been so busy. With his MCATs two weeks away, and making sure Gran had the best home care for when she left the hospital, his days were pretty full. Plus he picked up a few of the night shifts at the bar now that Sky had changed her hours. She spent the better part of her days working and when she wasn't she was hiring new staff and restructuring things at the bar now that she had a new partner. Once things settled there, she'd have more time to write, and for that he was happy.

He hadn't heard much from Caleb after his date with her. Basically the only thing he's said in a text was that it was... nice. He could only image he'd hear the details this weekend. Matt just hoped he planned to leave out the intimate ones, not that Caleb was a kiss-and-tell kind of guy. He wasn't. Neither of them were, which was why Caleb had no idea Matt had slept with Sky. Twice.

Fuck.

The roar of a speedboat engine had all the guys turning toward the dock. The motor stopped and the two girls who vacationed at the cottage down the road waved to them. They all waved back.

"Who's up for a ride?" one of the girls called out.

"Sure," Josh said, climbing to his feet.

"Yeah, why not," Jack said. He kicked Matt's foot. "Coming?"

Of course they'd all expect him to go. After all, he was the only other single in the group. "Can't. It's my birthday and I've got a beer to finish." Technically it wasn't his birthday until tomorrow, but whatever.

"I can't think of a better way to spend your birthday."

He could.

"The numbers don't add up, Jack. And I'm not sharing with you."

Jack laughed. "Worried you can't keep up?"

"More like you're my friend, and I'd hate to make you feel any less of a man." Matt shot back.

The guys all laughed.

"Tell you what. You stay here and think on that, while I go down there, and...not think about it."

The guys all laughed as Jack took off with Josh. Matt reached into the cooler and pulled out another beer. From the corner of his eye, he caught Cole watching him. In fact, he'd been studying Matt for the better part of the night.

"What?" he finally asked him.

Cole scrubbed his hand over her jaw. "That's what I was wondering."

"No idea what you're talking about," Matt said.

"You're all mopey," Cole said, channeling Gran. "I'm guessing it has something to do with Sky."

"Fuck off," he said and took another swig of beer to hide what he was really feeling.

"Then why didn't you take those girls up on the offer?"

"Like I said, the numbers didn't add up." He looked at the beer in his hands. "Plus I drank too much."

Turning the attention off him, Matt said, "So what do you think about Murph? Have you had a chance to work with him one-on-one yet?" Cole was the best damn handler of them all. A few years back he'd trained one of the smartest, yet most-undisciplined dogs at the shelter. Ralph was now working with a soldier here on American soil, and from all reports he was an expert at detecting leftover munitions.

"Yeah, I don't think he's cut out for bomb work."

Matt looked at the fire. "What will happen to him?"

"Actually, Gemma told me someone came in yesterday and wanted to adopt him."

His head jerked toward Cole, and while he was happy Murph was going to a good home, he knew he'd miss the guy. "Really?"

Across from him Garrett yawned. "I'm hitting the bed. Work calls early tomorrow."

"Yeah, I'm not too far behind," Matt said. He finished off his beer and climbed to his feet, feeling the effects from the alcohol. He made a quick trip to the bathroom, tore off all his clothes, then threw himself onto Caleb's comfortable bed. With the alcohol kicking his ass, he instantly fell asleep.

A noise at his door pulled him awake, and he rubbed his eyes in the dark trying to figure out what was going on. The door shut quietly and the mattress beside him sank.

"Hey," Sky said, her warm, familiar scent falling over him. But he caught another scent too, that of something sweet. What was going on?

He sat up and rubbed his eyes harder, waiting for them to adjust in the dark, but the room was pitch black and he couldn't see a damn things.

"Sky?" he croaked out his voice so hoarse from sleep he didn't even recognize it. "What—?"

"Shhh..."

A hand went to his chest to push him back down and the next thing he knew she was straddling him. He nearly bit off his tongue. What the fuck? Was Sky really here with him or was this some sort of wet dream.

The instant he felt her lips on his mouth, his neck, his chest...his cock, he lost all ability to think. A low groan crawled out of his throat and he pressed his hand to his forehead as she worked her tongue over him. Pleasure gathered in his core and breathing became a little harder.

One hand cupped his balls, as her head bobbed, taking

him in and out, and creating a rhythm that damn near had him exploding in her mouth. His muscles tensed, heat zinging through his body. She took him even deeper and when his crown hit the back of her throat, he gripped her hair and gave a little tug. Her excited moan resonated through his body.

He pulled her to him, and cupped her face, struggling to see her in the dark. "Sky," he murmured as her mouth closed over his. Her kiss was deep, sensual, full of emotion as she settled on top of him. Powerless to her seduction, his hands slid down her back, and with need and urgency pulling at him, he gripped her shirt and tugged. She broke the kiss and sat up, and his heart pounded harder as he listened to the soft rustle of her clothes as she undressed. She momentarily slid off him and he listened to the hiss of her zipper as she removed her pants.

His head began spinning and he wished he hadn't drank so much. But he couldn't think about that right now, because Sky grabbed something from the nightstand and climbed back over him.

"Open your mouth," she said.

"Sky?" Jesus, was that really him? His voice sounded so rough and gravelly.

"Cupcake," she whispered.

His lips parted and she put her finger into his mouth. The taste of buttery icing exploded on his tongue. He sucked her finger harder, and she moved on top of him, grinding that sweet pussy of hers on his stomach. Cock swelling to the point of agony, he slid his hand along her arm until he found the cupcake in her hand. The thought of spreading that icing on her body and licking it off had heat roaring through him. Wanting, no, needing, to lick and taste every inch of her, he took the cupcake and placed it beside them. He cupped her ass hard and in one fluid movement, flipped her over, pinning her beneath him. Her breathless gasp urged him on, and the need to touch her, taste her, ram his cock all the way inside her grew stronger than ever.

With her caged beneath him, he grabbed her hands in one of his and held them over her head. Sky writhed beneath him, her body aching for his touch. Using his free hand, he dipped his finger into the icing and said, "Open your mouth."

She obliged, and he put his finger in. She sucked him in deep, and his cock throbbed against her leg. "Mmm," she moaned, her tongue licking the last of the sugar away.

Hunger prowled through him as he dipped into the icing again, but this time he spread it on one nipple. Her body went tight beneath him, but instead of licking it off, he let the buttery frosting melt over her warm breast, let her revel in the sensation as it warmed and dripped down her breasts.

She sucked in a quick breath, and he held her hands tighter. "Please..." she cried out, her voice trembling slightly.

He lowered his head and swallowed a groan as he drew her nipple into his mouth. Heat and fire burned freely through his body as he laved her hard bud. Her nipple grew taut, and he nibbled on it, his cock growing harder as he clamped down.

Taking a big dollop of icing, he smeared it down her body, stopping when he reached her pubis. A cry lodged in her throat.

He put his mouth close to her ear, and there was a warning beneath his words when he said, "Keep your hands above your head."

Shifting positions, he let go of her hands and shimmied lower until he was between her legs. He gripped her thighs and widened them, and he felt the quiver that moved through her body. Falling over her, he put his hands on either side of her breasts and slowly licked a path downward, despite the fact that his cock was raging to get back inside her. With her body positioned perfectly, raw hunger nearly sucked the air from his lungs.

Her sweet moan as he lapped at the icing was music to his ears. He glanced up at her, wanting to see the heat in her eyes, but the room was too dark to see her. When he reached her pubis, he flattened himself on the mattress and shoved his hands beneath her to lift her slightly. Her aroused scent reached his nostrils, fueling the flames inside him. He spread her with his tongue, running the soft blade along her seam to widen her.

She rocked against him as he licked from bottom to top, his tongue landing firmly on her swollen clit. He took possession of her and greedily drew it into his mouth. Her legs hugged his head as his mouth pressed hungrily, taking her higher and higher. Her hips moved, and as he licked harder he could feel her soft quakes.

"Yes," she murmured as her body tightened. He lengthened his tongue and stroked softly as she came in his mouth. Her moans of ecstasy echoed in his head, filling him with a measure of satisfaction.

Infused with lust, he climbed up her body, and in one quick thrust, drove his cock all the way inside. He powered forward, burrowing deep, and she met each thrust, both taking as giving as pressure built. Jesus, it was good. So fucking good.

His hands found hers and their fingers linked as he slammed deep and fast. Some small part of his brain reminded him this was Sky and he needed to slow down, that he should be a little more gentle with her. But that thought left his mind as quickly as it had entered when he felt her climax a second time. Her wet heat scorched his cock, and when she moaned and clenched around his length, he knew he was done for. Succumbing to his needs, he drove inside and stilled as he let go, completely depleting himself.

He fell on top of her and let her hands go. They curled around his body, and with no thoughts left in his brain he pulled out and rolled off her. Sleep pulled at him. He grabbed Sky and drew her to his chest, and the next thing he knew she was covering them up with a blanket.

A long while later the sound of the guys rising in the cottage pulled him awake. He opened his eyes, snippets of last night coming back in bursts. His head jerked to the left, to look for Sky, but when he found her side of the bed empty, he pinched his eyes shut. Had he dreamt it? He opened his eyes again, and when he saw the cupcake on the nightstand, his heart jumped into his throat. Sky had been here and he'd slept with her.

He kicked the blankets off and tried to sort through the haze in his brain. Climbing to his feet he looked out his small window, and when he saw Sky at the dock, talking with Caleb, understanding slowly dawned. Holy Christ. She must have thought she was climbing into bed with Caleb.

Everything from anger, love, pain and possession raced through him, and when he saw Caleb pull her into his arms, everything he felt for her rushed to his heart and one thought filled his head: *Oh hell no!*

Sky was his. End of story. And it was well past time that he let everyone know it. Starting with her. He grabbed his clothes from the floor and climbed into them. Pulling open his bedroom door, he stormed out and when he found the others sipping coffee and staring at him, he left the cottage without saying a word.

He stomped down the path leading to the dock and when he reached it, both Sky and Caleb looked at him with surprise.

Sky opened her mouth to speak, but he shook his head to stop her. He reached for her hand and pulled her to him, and when those dark expressive eyes looked up at him, he cupped her face.

"I love you, Sky."

"I love you too," she said.

"No, you don't understand. I've loved you since the day you scraped your knee and threw a little dirt on it. You're not just the sky to me. You're my moon, my stars, my world. You're the toughest girl I know, yet the softest and the sweetest, and I need you in my life. But not as a friend."

"We can never be friends again, Matt."

"Sky, please, don't say that." Jesus, he needed her to listen, to understand. If he fucked things up between them... "I know you thought it was Caleb you crawled in with last night..." He stopped talking, took a breath and looked over her shoulder to find Caleb staring at him. "Caleb, I'm sorry. I thought...I wanted her to be happy. But I just...can't..." His gaze returned to her. "I'll do anything, whatever it takes to be worthy of you. Just please, tell me you'll give me a chance."

"Matt," she said quietly. "What are you taking about?"

He sucked in a quick breath and let it out slowly. "I'll be the kind of man you deserve, inside the bedroom and out."

Her hands closed over his as they cupped her face. "You're already that man. Don't you see, I knew it was you in that bed."

His heart missed a beat. "You did?"

"Of course I did. Caleb's truck wasn't here when I arrived last night, and I checked the boat to find it empty. That's when I figured you were sleeping in his room." A flush moved over her face, and she gave him a sweet, demure smile when she added, "The cupcake was part of your birthday present."

The sound of his throat working as he swallowed cut through the air. "But you..." He paused and looked at Caleb, taking in his smirk. "I woke up and saw you and Caleb together."

"No, you didn't," Caleb said. "And I'm getting out of here." He walked past them and headed toward the cottage.

"I don't get it," he said, staring deep into her eyes.

"You were sleeping so soundly, and I needed to talk to Caleb. I thought I'd be back before you woke up."

"Why did you need to talk to Caleb?"

"To explain how I feel."

This was all coming at him from left field, and his brain raced to catch up. "So you knew...it was me?"

"Let's get something straight," she said. "It doesn't matter to me if you're a field ambulance technician, a civilian medical doctor or a bouncer at Sky Bar. It's not what you do that matters to me, or makes you worthy." She poked him in the chest. "It's who you are in here."

"And who is that?" he asked.

"The man I love, which is why we can never go back to just being friends."

His throat closed up, making it hard to speak. "Sky—"

"You're everything I ever wanted in a man. Inside the bedroom and out. Our pretend relationship was supposed to open Caleb's eyes, but it opened mine instead. Caleb and I are friends, Matt, and that's all will ever be. You and me, however..."

"So you mean..."

"I mean, we should go back to bed and celebrate. Today is your birthday, right? And those cupcakes came in a package of twelve."

He shook his head, his heart filling with the love he felt for her. "I can't believe this. I'm the luckiest man in the world."

"And I'm the luckiest girl," she said, going up on her toes to press her lips to his. "Now, about your birthday. I didn't quite get any icing on your nose, and I believe I still owe you thirty spankings."

He put his arms around her and scooped her up, heat rushing to his groin. A gasp caught in her throat, and her eyes filled with love and desire when he said, "You are one bad little girl, and if anyone needs a spanking it's you."

He was about to carry her back to bed when the sound of a car door slamming reached his ears. "I like the sound of that, but first, I have another birthday present for you."

He frowned, having no idea what she was talking about, but then he heard barking. He set her back on her feet when Murphy came running down the dock toward him. He looked up to see Gemma waving to Sky.

He swallowed the lump pushing into his throat as he bent down on one knee to pet an excited Murphy. "Sky," he croaked out. "You were the one who adopted him."

A bird squawked in a nearby tree and Murphy took off running. They both laughed, and the humor fell from her face when he pulled her back into his arms. "If we're going to move into Gran's and make new memories, we can't do it without Murph, right?"

It took a moment for him to catch his breath again. "I love you, Sky. I love you so much. I want to live with you. I want to marry you. I want to make babies and have a house full of kids with you."

"Slow down," she said laughing. "Let's just celebrate your birthday first." She cupped his face, love shining in her eyes as her gaze moved over his. "But do know that I want all those things too."

"You are the sweetest girl I know."

She gave him a playful wink. "And here you just told me I was bad."

"Right," he said, scooping her back up again. "A bad girl who needs to be spanked..."

"Hey, it's your birthday, not mine."

"So you don't want me to spank you?"

Her face flushed. "Well..."

He grinned and started toward the cottage. "That's what I thought."

Thank You!

Thank you so much for reading, HIS BEST FRIEND'S GIRL, in my Line of Duty series. I hope you enjoyed the story! Be sure to check out the other 5 books in the series. Please keep reading for an excerpt of HIS REASON TO STAY.

His Obsession Next Door
    His Trouble in Tallulah
    His Taste of Temptation
    His Moment to Steal
    His Best Friend's Girl
    His Reason to Stay

Interested in leaving a review? Please do! Reviews help readers connect with books that work for them. I appreciate all reviews, whether positive or negative.

Happy Reading,
    Cathryn

AFTERWORD

Thank You!

Thank you so much for reading, HIS BEST FRIEND'S GIRL in my Line of Duty series. I hope you enjoyed the story as much as I enjoyed writing it. Be sure to check out the other 6 books in the series. Please keep reading for an excerpt of HIS REASON TO STAY.

- His Obsession Next Door
- His Strings to Pull (Novella)
- His Trouble in Tallulah
- His Taste of Temptation
- His Moment to Steal
- His Best Friend's Girl
- His Reason to Stay

Interested in leaving a review? Please do! Reviews help readers connect with books that work for them. I appreciate all reviews, whether positive or negative.

Happy Reading,
   Cathryn

HIS REASON TO STAY

Prologue

Rachel Andrews glanced at the clock, then turned her attention back to the patient in her chair. Christmas music filtered in through the speakers above as she grabbed the dental floss, and coiled it around anxious fingers. In two short hours she'd be picking James up at the airport and she was excited to have him home for the holidays. Truthfully, she hadn't seen much of him since he went off to Harvard right after their high school graduation two years ago. They might have started dating prom night, but she'd spent far more time with his younger brother, Kyle —before he enlisted in the army.

She continued with her cleaning, and thought about the two brothers who meant everything to her. After Rachel's dad had died of a massive heart attack, she and her mom had moved to Austin during Rachel's sophomore year. A friend had introduced her to James and she met Kyle through him. The three had instantly hit it off. They were all tight through high school, and in all honesty she loved both brothers equally. By the time their senior year came around, James became a little more possessive around her, and the two started dating before he went off to Harvard. A natural progression of their relationship, she supposed. While he was away, Rachel went to work at night to put herself through dental hygiene school, and Kyle, much to his parents' disappointment, joined the army the minute he was old enough. She wasn't sure why he wanted out of Austin so badly, only that he was eager to move away. God, she'd missed him so much, and when he upped and left after high school without so much as a goodbye, it nearly tore her apart.

Floss in hand, she swallowed down her emotions, finished the cleaning and straightened. "All set," she said. She removed the bib from around the woman's neck, and pressed a button to lift the chair. "Any plans for the rest of the day?" Rachel peeled off her gloves and tossed them onto the counter.

"Just finishing up some shopping."

Rachel groaned. She'd been so busy she hadn't even begun hers. Not that she had many people to buy for. Outside of her mother, the only family she had were James and Kyle. Not that the guys were related or anything. She and James had never even talked about a future. But they were both close to her heart and she'd be lost without them.

Her client stood, and Rachel walked her out to the front of the clinic. As she made her way to the counter to pay, Rachel hurried back to her station to clean it, ready to check out for the weekend. She said goodbye to the staff, grabbed her coat and rushed outside. She had just enough time to get home, shower, and change and make it to the airport on time.

The second she stepped outside and found Kyle leaning against his car waiting for her, her heart leapt. "Kyle," she squealed. She ran to him, and he picked her up, spinning her around as he hugged her tight. "What are you doing here?"

He grinned and set her back down, but kept his arms around her. "Oh, you know, just hanging out in front of the dentist's office because a guy never knows when he's going to chip a tooth."

Laughing, she hugged him tight, the warmth of his body chasing away the chill in the air. "I didn't even know you were home."

"Got back early."

"Your mom and dad must be excited to have the extra time with you." She fought off a shiver at the mention of his mom. No matter how hard she tried, she could never do anything right in Irene's eyes. Neither could Kyle.

"Haven't seen them yet."

Her heart gave a little start to know he'd come to see her first. God, how she'd missed him. His gaze moved over her face, then his eyes met hers. They held for an extra moment, then he let go of her and opened his car door.

"Get in. It's freezing out. I'll drive you home."

"I only live two blocks away." She slid into the car anyway, and he crossed the front and hopped in to the driver's seat. He grabbed the stick shift and she closed her hand over his. "James is getting in tonight. Will you be able to go to the airport with me? He'll be happy to see you."

He scoffed. "He's been gone for four months. It's not me he's going to be happy to see."

"Don't be crazy. Besides, I want you to come."

"I don't know, Rach."

Honest to God, she didn't want him out of her sight, for fear that he'd up and take off again. "Pleeeease...."

He smiled and shook his head. "You know I can never say no to you."

"Good." She relaxed into her seat as he pulled in to traffic and drove the short distance to the apartment she shared with her friend Sara, to cut costs.

He parked and they both darted up the stairs. Inside her small apartment, Kyle plunked himself down on her sofa and grabbed the remote. She glanced at him, noting how at home he seemed in her place. James hated her apartment. Said it was cramped and cluttered, but Kyle looked like he belonged.

"Give me a minue to shower and change." She darted down the hall, peeling her clothes off as she went. Twenty minutes later she emerged from her bedroom, wearing jeans and a sweater with a hint of makeup. Kyle climbed to his feet when he saw her and his glance moved down her body, a slow inspection that rippled through her blood.

Blue eyes locked back on hers and a muscle along his jaw ticked. "You look beautiful, Rach."

She laughed, but there was no humor in his eyes. "I bet you say that to all the girls."

"No just to you."

"Yeah, and the rest of the women you have falling at your feet." She wagged a finger at him. "I see how women look at you." He opened his mouth, like he wanted to say something, then shut it again. "Kyle?" she asked.

"We better get moving." He checked his watch. "Traffic is heavy."

She nodded, slipped on her boots and coat, and locked the door behind them. Kyle put his arm around her and offered his warmth when they stepped into the wind. Inside the car, she blasted the music and sang along to the Christmas carols. Kyle kept casting glances her way, grinning as she sang off tune. But she didn't care. She was happy. Her two favorite men were home, and that was the best Christmas present ever.

At the airport, Kyle parked and they dashed through the parking garage. She checked the board inside and clapped when she saw James's plane had arrived.

"Come on." She grabbed Kyle's hand. His big palm practically swallowed hers whole as she tugged him, maneuvering through the crowd until they reached the escalator. They stood at the bottom, and ten minutes later, she spotted James. His glance met hers and her heart beat faster when he gave her a big smile. That smile however, faltered a bit when he noticed his brother.

James reached them and she let go of Kyle's hand to give him a hug. He picked her up and spun her, in much the same manner as Kyle had earlier. His lips landed firmly on hers, kissing her possessively.

After a very public display of affection that made Rachel slightly uncomfortable, James put his hand on Kyle's shoulder. "Hey, little brother, good to see you."

"You too." Kyle threw his arms around James and gave him a hug. A noise sounded at the luggage carousel and Kyle inched back. "I'll grab your bag for you and give you two a minute." Rachel smiled. That was just like Kyle. Always watching out for his older brother and conscious of his needs. There wasn't anything Kyle wouldn't do for him.

As James pulled her in close, she cast a glance at Kyle, who suddenly couldn't seem to meet her eyes.

James shifted his backpack. "No need. I packed light. Let's get out of here." They started toward the car, Kyle walking a few feet ahead of them to give her and James a bit of privacy, she assumed. James leaned in to her. "I made reservations for us at Lucien's."

She blinked, surprised. Lucien's was a very expensive restaurant, and she was far from dressed properly. Not to mention a meal there probably cost more than she made in a day. "You did?"

"I wanted to go straight there."

Her brow furrowed. "You don't want to go home first?"

"No."

Rachel looked him over. He seemed anxious about something. "Is everything okay?"

"Yeah, I just didn't expect to see you with Kyle, and the reservation is for two."

"I asked him to come. Do you think we can change it to three?" She didn't want to leave Kyle out.

"Hey," Kyle said, slowing to let them catch up. "You two go ahead to dinner. I have things to do anyway."

She put her hand on his arm. "But I want you to come."

"Yeah, me too," James said. The brothers exchanged a look Rachel didn't understand.

"You sure?" Kyle asked.

"Yeah, I think you should come. You should be there."

Rachel wasn't sure what James meant by that, but she was happy that they were all going to be together. James pulled his phone from his pocket and called the restaurant as they made their way to the car.

The brothers sat in the front, catching up with one another, and Rachel claimed the back seat. She sat there grinning, her heart so full she was unable to wipe the smile from her face.

Thirty minutes later, they were led to a quiet table in the back of the restaurant, and James ordered a bottle of wine. As they sipped, his hand closed over hers, and across from her Kyle shifted in the seat.

"It's good to be home." James leaned in to press his lips to hers. This time she was the one shifting. Sure they were dating, but it felt oddly wrong kissing James in front of Kyle, and James seemed to be showing more affection in front of his brother than usual. His lips lingered and he coiled his fingers in her hair. "I missed you so much." Before she could answer, James pushed his chair back, and then he went down on one knee.

Rachel gasped and her gaze instantly shot to Kyle. He sat ramrod straight in his chair, his eyes locked on hers, his mouth set in a grim line.

"Rachel," James said, a note of irritation in his voice. "Look at me."

She turned her attention to James, her heart pounding so hard in her ears, she could barely hear anything.

He pulled a box from his pocket and tears pricked her eyes. Was this really happening? Here, in front of Kyle? Is this what he wanted his brother to see?

"Will you marry me?" he asked.

"Oh, my God," she said under her breath. Once again her gaze crept to Kyle's. The muscles along his jaw ticked, and his Adam's apple bobbed as he swallowed hard. Her throat tightened, her vision going a little fuzzy around the edges.

She blinked, and something in Kyle's face softened. There was a slight nod of his head as he pushed back in his seat. As he distanced himself both physically and emotionally, she turned back to James and knew she had her answer.

ABOUT CATHRYN

New York Times and *USA today* Bestselling author, Cathryn is a wife, mom, sister, daughter, and friend. She loves dogs, sunny weather, anything chocolate (she never says no to a brownie) pizza and red wine. She has two teenagers who keep her busy with their never ending activities, and a husband who is convinced he can turn her into a mixed martial arts fan. Cathryn can never find balance in her life, is always trying to find time to go to the gym, can never keep up with emails, Facebook or Twitter and tries to write page-turning books that her readers will love.

Connect with Cathryn:
Newsletter
https://app.mailerlite.com/webforms/landing/c1f8n1
Twitter: https://twitter.com/writercatfox
Facebook:
https://www.facebook.com/AuthorCathrynFox?ref=hl
Blog: http://cathrynfox.com/blog/
Goodreads:
https://www.goodreads.com/author/show/91799.Cathryn_Fox

Pinterest http://www.pinterest.com/catkalen/

ALSO BY CATHRYN FOX

Deep Desire

Private Pleasure

Captured and Claimed Series:

Yours to Take

Yours to Teach

Yours to Keep

Firefighter Heat Series

Fever

Siren

Flash Fire

Playing For Keeps Series

Slow Ride

Wild Ride

Sweet Ride

Breaking the Rules:

Hold Me Down Hard

Pin Me Up Proper

Tie Me Down Tight

Stand Alone Title:

Hands on with the CEO

Torn Between Two Brothers

Holiday Spirit

Unleashed

Knocking on Demon's Door

Web of Desire

Printed in the USA
CPSIA information can be obtained
at www.ICGtesting.com
LVHW042031270924
792325LV00037B/631